Persephone

Persephone

KITTY THOMAS

Burlesque Press

Printed in the United States of America

ISBN-13: 978-1-938639-38-8
ISBN-10: 1-938639-38-3

Wholesale orders can be placed through Ingram.
Published by Burlesque Press

contact: burlesquepress@nym.hush.com

For M.

Acknowledgments

Thank you to the following people for their help with Persephone:

Robin Ludwig @ gobookcoverdesign.com for the gorgeous cover art and for the badass bookmarks!

Thank you to Michelle and Karen for beta work!

Thank you to Cathy for copyedits. I'm terrible at commas.

And thank you to M for digital formatting! Love you!

Dear Readers,

Persephone and Hades is my favorite myth, which, if you've read many of my books probably isn't a huge shocker. I've read probably every version out there and now here is my version of it. If you are familiar with classical mythology, you will realize that I've taken several liberties with various aspects of the story as well as some aspects of the underworld.

The biggest difference is the absence of Demeter. Nearly every version of the myth somehow ends up making what should be Persephone's story about "how her mother has suffered". Demeter so strongly overshadows everything that I removed her entirely so Persephone can have her say.

I hope you enjoy my retelling of this myth.

Thank you for reading and supporting my work!

Kitty ^.^

If you enjoy this title, you might also enjoy: Submissive Fairy Tales, Blood Mate, and The Last Girl.

For full title list and to subscribe to my new release list, visit: kittythomas.com

One

"I don't know how you do that. It's damn near magical," Lynette said as she stared in wonder. "Do what?"

"That." She pointed at all the flowers around the shop as if this should be obvious to any thinking person. "The way you take nearly dead broken things and bring them back to life. I've never seen anything like it."

"Oh," Persephone said. "I don't know. You just have to listen to them. They tell you what they need, but they speak very quietly. It's hard to hear them in the city."

The Perfect Posie was a quaint flower shop situated between an authentic Italian sausage shop and an old vinyl record store. It wasn't exactly the quietest or best place for plant life to flourish in Persephone's opinion, but she worked with what she had.

Lynette shook her head, her long, dark curls falling behind her back, hiding a black raven tattoo on her shoulder. "Fine. Don't tell me. I'm going to lunch; do you want anything?"

"No. I had a big breakfast this morning." It was a lie, but if she admitted she hadn't had anything but coffee, Lynette would start mothering her.

"If you don't eat something, you'll blow away."

"I'll have something later. I'm fine."

Lynette slipped out of the shop into the bustling New York City streets, leaving Persephone with her flower arranging. Her boss was right; the lilacs had been wilted and nearly dead when they'd arrived that morning. Lynette had been about to make an angry phone call to her supplier and order more when Persephone had taken them to a back room and just . . .

What exactly had she done with them? She wasn't sure. She gave them some flower food and water and sunlight and talked to them a little. It was what you were supposed to do. She just did it, and they'd come back. It wasn't magic. It was common sense and patience and love. You had to love them, or the spark of life wouldn't come back. But every time she did it, Lynette had acted as if it was something close to a goddamn miracle.

She sighed and left the lilacs to do whatever healing it was they needed from their arduous trip to the store and stepped outside for some air.

Persephone had been promised a beautiful perfect day today by everyone. The weather man, her chiropractor neighbor, even the bees had seemed to be in agreement, but instead, what she'd come to work in was an ugly overcast day with heavy oppressive clouds that seemed to push down on the city until it almost felt smaller somehow.

Now the sky was clear and blue and perfect with only a few wispy clouds that hadn't seen fit to leave yet. Each time she'd looked out the window, she'd seen a little more hope in the forecast. But she'd never seen the clouds move. They'd instead seemed to unobtrusively melt and disappear into the sky.

It was the least foreboding day one could imagine. And yet.

The hairs on the back of her neck prickled and stood on edge as if zapped by a jolt of static electricity. Across the street, she spotted a nondescript black sedan.

It's probably a bookstore customer or somebody who works in the area.

But she couldn't shake the overwhelming paranoia that the sedan was here for her. It felt like death coming to claim her. A long, slow shiver whispered down her spine. *Just a breeze.* But she wasn't convinced.

She went back into the flower shop and to the back room and sat next to the vase of lilacs now blooming happily in a patch of sunlight. She felt as though she were huddling. Hiding. But from what? This was so ridiculous.

The bell over the flower shop door jangled.

"Hello?"

It was a deep, gravelly male voice. It was a melody, a song. It was the kind of voice that would lead you over a cliff if you followed it. And yet Persephone got up off the stool she was perched on and stepped out into the main room.

"C-can I help you?"

The stranger turned. He wore a black suit with a black linen shirt underneath. It was clearly professionally tailored. Not off the rack. It fit too perfectly. He had dark olive skin, eyes black as coal, and hair that was the same. He had hands that . . . could crush you.

Persephone pushed that thought away.

Every inch of him was perfect, but that smile. It promised evil things.

While Persephone had never seen the car door across the street open, she somehow knew this man had come out of that black sedan. He was the thing that made her hair stand on end. He was the thing that made her hide in a back room with a vase of flowers as if it could protect her.

"Persephone." Her name rolled off his tongue like a prayer. "You have no idea how long I've been looking for you."

"How do you know my name?" Somehow, she'd made that whole sentence come out without a stutter. As it was, she was gripping the counter, her knuckles turning white—doing all her panicking for her. But her voice remained a mask of calm. For some reason, she knew the last thing she could give this man was her fear.

He would enjoy it too much.

"I've known your name for centuries. And truth be told, the rest of the world should have known it as well, my little goddess of spring."

Okay. This man was crazy. He spoke in riddles. Obviously, he hadn't known her name for centuries, and what was this goddess of spring nonsense? Did that pick-up line really work with other women? To know her name, he had to have been stalking her. Watching her.

Persephone eased her way toward the register end of the counter where there was a comforting heavy, round panic button situated under the Formica. In the city, you never knew who might come in or what they might want. It wasn't unheard of for some meth head to burst in demanding the money from the register of small shops like this.

Her finger eased closer to the button.

"I wouldn't," the stranger said. "Don't disappoint me now."

"I-I think you need to leave."

"Yes, we both do." He stretched out a hand toward her. "Come along, then."

Persephone took several steps back. "I'm not going anywhere with you. I don't know you!" She tried to reassure herself that she was safe. The city was alive with activity. Plenty of witnesses. It was a bright sunny day outside. The birds were chirping. And he hadn't pulled out a gun or anything.

He smiled. It didn't help. "I'm sorry. You are everything I thought you would be. I've forgotten my manners in the midst of my pleasant surprise. I'm Hades."

"That's a name?" Didn't it mean something like Hell? Who named their kid that? There was something else prickling at the edge of her awareness. She'd heard this name in a bigger context but couldn't remember now in all the edging hyperventilation.

"Oh, you must have read about me. I'm renowned. It's a little story from Greece. Hades, god of the underworld? I know they must still be teaching about me in school, even if they gloss over all the fun bits."

That's where she'd heard the name. Years ago in school.

And no, they hadn't glossed over the fun bits. At least she could be grateful this guy was just crazy and not actually Hades. When she'd learned mythology she'd thought that particular god had a rather dark reputation as well as a singular obsession with the queen he never found.

This guy was hot, no doubt, but calling himself a god . . . well, it was a bit self-aggrandizing. And yet, somehow, she didn't think he was just being vain. He really believed this insanity.

He sighed. "Your father has been hiding you from me for thousands of years."

"My father?"

"Zeus."

A hysterical laugh bubbled to the surface. Her father was a farmer out in Idaho—definitely not Zeus. She hadn't seen her dad in a couple of years. Not since her mother died.

Hades moved then, so fast she could hardly catch her breath. All at once, he was standing right next to her, his hand forming a death grip on her arm, dragging her from the flower shop.

She'd hoped while he was sharing all the details of his delusional fantasies that a customer would come in, maybe a cop. Hell, she'd take a mafia goon—anyone who could get this guy to go away. But no one had come.

Out on the street, suddenly, all was quiet. Nothing. No one. Lime-green spring leaves fluttered in breezes on the trees lining the street, and clouds began to gather again, darkening the sky as he pulled her across the road to his waiting car.

There was no traffic. How could there be no traffic? No pedestrians. It was as if the city of New York, or at least this one street of it, had become a ghost town.

Persephone let out a blood curdling shriek. But the only response was a flock of birds flying away from her. And now she was utterly alone. With him.

She struggled and tried to squirm out of his grasp, but his grip was unyielding, her efforts laughable.

This wasn't real. I-it couldn't be. This wasn't how the world worked. Persephone willed herself to wake up. But the reality in front of her stubbornly remained. Solid and unyielding.

Hades pushed a button on a key remote, and the doors to the sedan unlocked. He ignored her continued struggles and walked her calmly around to the passenger side. "Get in."

"N-no."

"Persephone, don't try my patience further. Get in the car."

"No! If you're going to kill me, you can do it right here." In the middle of a city street where somehow all the people had disappeared and the perfect blue sky had turned dark and gray within minutes.

He looked at her as if he found her amusing. "You think I'd search for you this long and then just kill you? That's the kind of thing a human would do. You need to start thinking more like the immortal that you are."

She'd always known there were a lot of crazy people running around the city, but this guy . . . well she'd never really thought that crazy could come in such an otherwise polished package wrapped in a nice suit and good looks and a clean, shiny car.

But here he was.

After another moment, he opened the door and shoved her in. Before she could try to escape, he was somehow already in the driver's side. The door locks clicked ominously into place.

"I've got child locks," he said, to save her the energy of trying to open her own door.

Oh god. Oh god. Oh god.

"Yes?" he said, amused.

Oh. She must have said that out loud. She thought she'd only been thinking it. The terror had become so all consuming that she wasn't sure which thoughts were still safely sequestered in her head and which ones had escaped her mouth into the space between her and her insane captor.

Tears slid down her cheeks. "Please. Y-you need help. You don't know what you're doing. I-is there some medicine you should be taking? Do you have a doctor we can call?"

Hades shook his head. "My poor spring goddess. Soon enough you will believe me."

"You can still let me go."

"Never."

That one word was absolute. Final.

Persephone tried to breathe normally. Tried to think. But she couldn't. All she could do was cry. There was no reasoning with a crazy person. If he hadn't been so mentally unhinged then . . . maybe.

As Hades started the car and pulled out onto the road, she realized there was something cold and dead and broken inside him. The temperature of the car seemed to have dropped just from him being in it. If only Lynette's belief that she had magic were true. If only she did have some power to awaken and bring dead things to life. But, of course, that was as much fantasy as the story the man beside her had concocted.

She didn't know what was broken inside this man's brain, but it would do no good to make up her own fantasies. She thought at least one of them should remain sane.

At the end of the road, Hades turned onto another street. This one had people on it. And all at once, the sense of unreality from before faded. Rain had started to come down in pelting sheets. People hid underneath yellow and green and black and pink umbrellas, darting down the sidewalks with their heads down.

Despite the rain, the traffic moved at an easy pace like the red sea parting for them, delivering Persephone up to whatever dark fate awaited her.

Thunder cracked in the distance. The windshield wipers clicked gently back and forth. Finally, Hades broke his silence. "I wish I could comfort you and tell you I'm not going to hurt you, that you'll be safe with me. But I don't want to make promises I can't keep."

Another strangled sob escaped her control. Her hands had started shaking on her lap. But otherwise, she was silent. She had to think. There would be a moment. She had to wait for that moment so she could get away.

Then, as if Hades hadn't as much as admitted he planned to hurt her, he said, "That hair. It's like sunshine. So pale and blonde and glimmering. And your skin . . . it's so fair with that beautiful flush of color in your cheeks, and crystal blue eyes, pure like a lake." How long was he going to wax poetic like this? He left one hand on the steering wheel while his other encircled her wrist. "And these tiny fragile bones. Like birds. You're everything I imagined the goddess of spring would be, like a ripe, young bud the moment before full bloom. It's hard to believe you're indestructible."

Despite his coldness, Persephone's skin felt burned under his touch.

She took a long, deep breath. "Please, you have to believe me. I'm not who you think I am. Whatever you believe about yourself, you can't bring me into it. I'm not indestructible. I'm human. I'm fragile. I will break. I will die."

Hades released her wrist and shook his head, a look of disgust on his face. "Your fucking father. You may very well break under my hands. But you won't die."

"Where are you taking me?"

"To the underworld. Where else?"

Okay, where was he really taking her? Some dank basement somewhere? A mysterious concrete compound? A cabin in the woods? Where did a guy like this like to hole up? It was a really nice car. And a really nice, well-tailored suit. This guy, crazy or not, had some money. And that scared her. It was bad enough to be kidnapped by a crazy man. It was far worse to be taken by one with resources.

He stopped in front of the Empire State Building. There was an empty space right there in front of the building for him to park. What? Persephone shook herself again. Why was he stopping here, and why on earth was there just some place for his car, as if by magic? No. She was not going to be sucked into his delusion.

"This is our stop, Sunshine. We go on foot from here to the portal."

"But what about your car?"

"It's not my car."

Hades got out and came around to her side, helping her out of the car that wasn't his car. No people again outside. The rain was still coming down hard. Maybe they were all inside, sheltering in place.

He gripped her wrist again and led her into the building. To her absolute and utter delight, there were people inside. Crowds and crowds. And security. She was going to get away from this guy. It was all going to be okay.

"Help me! This man kidnapped me. He's crazy!"

But no one moved to help her. No one even turned when she screamed.

"I thought you might try that. You can scream all you want. They can't hear you. They can't see you," Hades said. He wasn't even ruffled.

"H-how? How is this happening?" *Just a few more minutes. I'll wake up.*

"I told you I'm a god. My will is always obeyed. Something you will learn very soon."

Despite the ineffectiveness, Persephone continued to scream for help. Still no one noticed her. No one noticed that a handsome, swarthy lunatic was dragging her through the building while she fought and struggled and screamed.

"I'd hate for you to wear yourself out this early," Hades said. "You're going to need all your energy where we're going." He dragged her down a hallway to a service elevator.

An employee followed in behind them and pushed the button to the very top. The 102nd floor.

"We're going to 103," Hades said, conversationally.

"What? There is no 103rd floor."

"Oh yes there is. It's a secret floor for celebrities and gods."

Persephone ignored that craziness and turned to the employee. "Hey! Help me! Can't you see me? You have to help me get away from this man." She was screaming at the top of her voice, but still the employee seemed as though he were deaf or ignoring her as he watched the buttons light up on the way to the top.

She hauled back and punched the guy in the shoulder. He jumped, rubbed his shoulder and looked around, spooked.

Hades grabbed her around the waist and pulled her back into the corner. "Now, now. That's not nice. I only shielded for sound and vision."

He was too uncomfortably close. Persephone felt enveloped by him. And for the first time, she felt he was something other than crazy. He was something dark and powerful and determined. She felt a hard block of muscle pressed against her back as he held her close to his chest.

The employee's eyes darted around the elevator, unable to see that a big, terrifying man was holding someone captive mere feet from him. He turned back to the panel and pushed a button for a lower floor. The elevator stopped a moment later, and the guy couldn't scramble off fast enough.

When the doors closed again, and the elevator resumed its ascent, Hades released his hold on Persephone. She backed away to the farthest corner from him and squeezed her eyes shut, trying to block everything out. Could this man actually have some legitimate magic powers? She felt crazy even thinking it. No. It's a dream. When she woke up, she'd spend the whole day laughing about this. Lynette would love this story.

And yet . . . until she woke, all of this felt a little too real.

The elevator stopped at the observation deck. Hades dragged her out and took her to the right and pushed her through another door so fast she didn't have time to scream at this set of tourists for help. Now they were in the belly of the building—the secret parts no one ever saw. She didn't see another balcony. Instead he pulled her through a labyrinth of pipes and electricity boxes.

"Climb," he ordered pointing to a terrifyingly tight steel thing that was halfway between a stairway and a ladder.

She shook her head frantically. "I-I can't. Please, I can't." It was just too high. When he'd first dragged her onto the elevator, she'd thought they were going to the top observation deck, which though frightening, was enclosed by a safety fence. What if there was no fence where he was taking her?

"Go! I'm right behind you."

As if there were any reality in which that could be a comfort. She did all she could do under the circumstances. She climbed.

At the top, her worst fears were confirmed. It was a cramped balcony with a railing only a couple feet tall around it. She could easily stumble over it to her death. Or be pushed.

"Please take me back down. Please. I'm not her. I swear I'm not."

If possible, the sky had grown even darker, nearly black as if it had become night already. The only light came every few moments as lighting streaked by, thunder chasing at its heels.

"We have to jump," he said.

"Jump?" She couldn't back away from him. There was nowhere to back to, except over that tiny ledge.

Persephone had already returned to denial about the things she'd seen. The silent street. The crowds who couldn't see or hear her. She couldn't have seen what she thought. It just wasn't possible. Now she was back to: crazy man wants to jump off the Empire State Building—and drag her along for the ride.

When she spoke again, her voice shook so much she couldn't believe she could get the words out. "P-please, you have to listen to me. We can get you help. I know this feels real to you, but . . . we will die if we jump. And I know you don't want that."

He laughed. "I can't believe you still think I'm insane. The glamor around us wasn't a big enough clue for you? This mortal Kool Aid you've drunk must be pretty powerful stuff. But not powerful enough."

He grabbed her hand and brought her to the ledge. Her heart pounded in her chest and head and throat as she stood with him looking down from dizzying heights to the street far below them.

"Scared of heights?"

"Y-yes," she gasped. She tried to pull out of his grip to get away from the edge. No amount of self talk that she'd wake up seemed to be penetrating the fear now.

"I hear exposure is the best cure." And then he jumped, pulling her with him over the side of one of the tallest buildings in the city.

As she fell, everything switched to slow motion while her life flashed before her eyes. And then, in the moment before impact, she had the sick realization that death would definitely take her to the underworld if such a place existed.

But she never hit concrete. Instead, her hand slipped out of his, and a couple of moments later, she splashed into a cold, black sea inside some kind of cavern. Persephone didn't have time to contemplate the impossibility of this outcome because the water was trying to pull her under to drown her. It seemed angry at being disturbed by her unceremonious falling into it.

A hand reached down and pulled her out, soaked and shivering. "I told that fucking idiot to have the boat ready for us when we came through the portal."

But there was a boat now—a small, dark, wooden row boat. Hades pulled Persephone into it. She clung to him for a moment like a half-drowned rat trying to get her bearings. Then when she realized whose arms she'd sought safety in, she pulled away quickly and moved to the far end of the boat. Hades didn't comment or try to stop her retreat. Why would he? It wasn't like she could go very far.

The water had smoothed and calmed now; the only ripples were the oars as he rowed them across this mysterious black sea. Neither of them spoke as Hades rowed. Persephone felt she must be in shock. She felt cold and unreal. But she couldn't deny what was right in front of her eyes. Not anymore.

"A-am I dead?"

He chuckled. "No. Though that is the normal way of it. There are few living beings down here, but you are not dead."

So if she wasn't dead, and this wasn't a dream . . . Despite the growing unlikelihood, Persephone continued to hope that she would wake up in her bed, maybe late for work, but safe in the sunlight. Maybe that forecast of a perfect day she'd been promised would happen from the first morning bird chirp until the sun went down. She and Lynette would laugh about it at the flower shop.

But even as she tried to hold onto these last frail bits of hope, a deeper, darker part of her knew that Hades was real. This place was real. She wasn't sure if he was a god or a demon, but he was definitely something supernatural. And she was beginning to believe him when he said he was immortal. But it still didn't mean he wasn't crazy. If he lived down here . . . well it wasn't exactly in the sanity guidebook. One might easily lose their mind down here. Maybe Hades had, too. Either way, she was just a regular person, and she had to make him understand that.

"Ummm, Hades?"

He looked up from the rowing. "Yes?"

"I . . . I believe you are who you say you are . . ."

He chuckled. "Well, how noble of you to throw me that small bone."

"I . . . I mean . . . unless I'm dreaming. But I'm not her. Whoever you're looking for, it's not me. I'm just a human."

A red, fiery glow came into his eyes, and she thought she heard him growl. A moment later, he seemed to have composed himself, and his eyes went back to the rich, coal black of before.

"Everything will be explained."

And that was that. He didn't speak another word to her for the duration of their trip across the water. After a long time, they reached a dock. Hades got out and helped her out. He led her to a large, black gate that looked like massive gnarled tree limbs had been transformed into metal.

This time he didn't grip her arm so hard. There was no need to. Where was she going to go? She had no idea how to get out of this place. And the water here wanted her dead. Maybe it knew she shouldn't be down here in the dark. It wasn't natural.

Just inside the gate stood a giant monster with three heads. Persephone drew back.

"It's only Cerberus, my dog."

"T-that's a dog? But it's huge. And it's got three heads," she said as if these facts must have escaped Hades' notice when he picked the pup up at the evil pet store.

But then the giant thing started to bark out of the mouths of two of its heads. The other head was busy panting happily. A tail thumped hard and fast on the ground in excitement, sending off tremors like a small earthquake.

"Settle down, boy," Hades said as the dog bent down to be petted, each of the three heads fighting for the attention of its master.

"Will he bite?" Persephone asked, still keeping a minimum safe distance from the giant beast.

Hades looked back at her. "Cerberus? This silly thing? Of course not." But then his expression turned dark. "Unless you try to escape the underworld. Then he might eat your face."

Persephone couldn't be sure if he was kidding or not, but from his serious expression, she thought not. And she very much didn't want to test it to find out. She edged closer.

When she got within striking distance, a giant tongue came out of a giant head and licked the side of her face.

"Cerberus, stop that!" Hades said.

The monstrous dog stopped slobbering all over her, and Hades extended a hand. This time she took it. He led her past the big guard dog and down a long tunnel lit by torch light.

She wasn't prepared at all for what lay on the other side of the tunnel. It looked like a glittering dark kingdom. They stood inside what appeared to be a giant cavern. Only she saw a black sky overhead with thousands of shining stars and a big full moon.

"It's not the real moon, or sky, or stars. It's just a glamor. More magic."

"Is it always like this?"

"If you're asking if there is a magic sun to go with it, no. There are rules in the underworld that even I must follow. It's always night here." He said this with some sadness, and something inside her constricted for a moment.

A small distance away there was a castle. It was made out of some black glittering stone that almost seemed to glow in the moonlight.

Hades led her down hundreds of steps, deeper into the cavern where a heavy, terrifying fog seemed as though it might smother them. But Hades was untroubled by the fog. They only walked a short distance until they reached the mouth of a forest of dead trees that formed a tangle of gnarled branches. Tethered to one of the trees were two large, black horses.

"At least they managed to follow one instruction properly," Hades said as he untied the horses. "It's quicker by horseback."

Persephone felt as though every step she took and every second that passed she was being more deeply ensnared into a dark world she might never escape, but Hades waited patiently for her to move closer to the horse he'd assigned her. He helped her up into the saddle, got on his own horse, and then they were off.

She leaned in close to the horse's mane, bracing herself against the branches that tried to jump out and snag her. Hades' horse was just up ahead, moving much faster than hers. Yet hers obviously had its orders and knew where to go, and there was no diverting it from its mission.

They reached the end of the dead forest and came upon a vast meadow where nothing grew—only a sea of tall, dead, brown grass that swayed in the breeze she knew couldn't be a real breeze. In the meadow, the fog cleared away to reveal the moonlight and the glittering castle again just up ahead.

When she reached the castle, Hades was already getting off his horse and giving it to someone. Or something. Persephone wasn't sure if the groom was human or some sort of demon. Dead or alive.

Hades helped her off her horse and passed those reins to the groom as well, then he led her up a set of black marble stairs and into the castle.

Guards lined the long entry hall, gazes straight ahead. They wore heavy armor, and again, Persephone couldn't be sure if they were human or demon. Dead or alive. She found herself gripping Hades' hand harder because the one thing that was becoming increasingly clear to her was that there could be no way out of this place, no escape from her captor.

And if possible, Hades somehow seemed like the least scary thing down here and the only one who might have enough interest to protect her.

A gleaming silver rug glowed like the moonlight and extended the full length of the hall, lighting their way. Hades led her to the end, then he turned left and took her down a set of gray stone steps that spiraled downward for what seemed like forever.

Down below was a large room encased entirely in stone. Torches lined the walls. The room seemed mostly empty except for a large cage in the center.

Persephone jolted out of the disorienting fog she'd been in. As she truly realized what was happening, reality seemed to snap and make a long metallic grinding sound. No, that was the cage door opening. Hades flung her in and slammed the door shut and locked it.

Then he turned without a word and went back up the stairs.

"Hades! Don't leave me down here, please!" She couldn't think what she could have done for this to happen. Had he just meant to take her and lock her in a cage forever? Why?

She sat on the ground and drew her legs up to her chest. Her jeans and T-shirt were still damp from the water she'd been in. And now this cold, dank dungeon. She was going to freeze to death. She was going to die down here. She'd never see the sun again.

Persephone began to cry. She cried so hard and so long that she didn't hear Hades come back downstairs.

"Eat," he ordered.

She looked up and wiped the tears off her face to see him holding a deep red fruit out to her through the bars. He'd sliced it open. It looked juicy and delicious and inviting. How could he get fruit down here when nothing grew?

"What is it?"

"Insurance," he said.

"What?"

"A pomegranate. If you ever want to leave this cage, you'll eat."

"Please tell me why I'm here. I don't understand any of this. Please."

His eyes glowed again. "Eat first."

Was he drugging her? Why was he so insistent? There was something wrong about this. She knew there must be, but she was getting hungry, and she was so tired and cold. If this might get her out of the cage . . .

"Eat!" he growled.

Persephone reached out and took the pomegranate from his hand and plucked out one of the seeds. She closed her eyes and ate one. She expected to die. But nothing tragic happened. So she ate several more.

She opened her eyes to find Hades smiling at her—that gorgeous, evil smile that couldn't mean anything good.

"Now you're mine, tied here forever. It doesn't matter what your father does now. You are *mine*."

She felt the trap close over her as the pomegranate fell from her hand. The sound of the fruit hitting the ground was deafening as seeds and juice spilled out to stain the stone like blood.

"W-what do you mean?"

"My sweet, innocent little goddess. There is a part of me very glad you were fooled into believing you were human. You couldn't know that eating pomegranate seeds in the underworld would link you to me and this place forever. Well, now you know."

"Hades . . . please. I'm cold. Don't leave me in the cage." She couldn't deal right now with the prospect of forever. She could only handle dealing with the immediate circumstances of being locked in a cage.

"I have things to say first. And you will listen."

She didn't argue, too afraid to. Persephone was back to believing he was mad. He must be. And she'd been in this place too long now to really believe she was dreaming anymore. Somehow . . . this was real.

He paced around the outside of the cage, looking quite agitated as he told her a story he must have held inside for a very long time.

"There was a prophecy. You were destined to be mine. But your selfish father found out about it from a seer when you were born. And he couldn't allow that, not his sweet, beautiful daughter down here in the dark with me.

"Zeus has the upper world. Poseidon has the sea. What do I have? Darkness and death. Your father couldn't let me have one beautiful, bright, warm thing. Not one. He took your powers and hid you away in the mortal world. When I learned of his deception, it still took me centuries to find you. He'll find you, too. My magic won't hide you forever. He probably already knows where you are. But it's too late. And now he will know it as well."

"My father is a farmer in Idaho. H-he's not a god."

"That's not your father. Zeus gave you fake memories. He keeps moving you around so people don't figure out you don't age and altering all the memories, including yours. Spiteful bastard."

"No. I-it's not true. I'm just a person."

Hades unlocked the cage and stepped inside. Persephone backed away, suddenly more uncomfortable than ever with his nearness.

"I think we should send daddy a package. What do you think? A finger? I bet he'd like a finger."

Persephone's eyes widened. She was still convinced Hades had the wrong woman. This goddess he was talking about couldn't be her. But at this point, playing along with the crazy god seemed like the smartest response.

"H-Hades . . . why did you want me? Surely not to cut me into pieces." She hoped.

He withdrew a gleaming silver knife from his pocket. "Oh, don't worry. I told you you're indestructible. It'll grow back."

He was really going to do this. She took a couple more steps away from him until the black, hard metal of the cage pressed against her back.

"No! Please . . .n-no. Don't. I-I'll do whatever you want. Don't do this." She dropped to her knees, begging him. The tears flowed down her cheeks. "Hades, please. I-I'll be yours. Forget my father. Don't . . ."

Something in his expression softened the smallest fraction. Then he growled and left the cage, slamming and locking it behind him. He flung the silver knife to the far corner of the dungeon, well outside her reach, and then left her there.

Persephone moved to the center of the cage, shivering from cold and fear. She was too afraid to call for him again.

Two

Hades paced on the upper level. He hadn't made it beyond the entry hall before he'd started. He could hear her crying all the way up here. Damn her tears. He'd had every intention of sending Zeus a finger all wrapped up in a black box with a silver satin bow. Maybe he'd send more than one. Maybe he'd send the same one every day for a year.

It *would* grow back after all. It truly was no big deal. But it would drive that control freak father of hers insane. That was the important part. And it would hurt. Zeus had kept her protected and bubble wrapped, shielded from her fate. She probably hadn't suffered a day in her long life. That was about to change. And she had her father to thank for it.

"Umm, My Lord?" One of the guards had left his post.

Hades rounded on him and snarled. "What?"

"M-my Lord do you think it wise to keep her down there like that?"

"She won't die."

"No, but . . . remember what the seer said."

Hades went back to pacing. He was going to wear a hole in the glowing silver rug at this rate.

When he'd discovered Zeus's duplicity, he'd gone to his own seer to confirm the story. She'd said Persephone was meant to be his queen.

And here he was treating her like his prisoner. But could she not be both? While he had felt the slightest twinge of something that had stopped him from cutting her finger off, her tears and begging wouldn't stop all his plans.

Just being near her, he wanted to dominate her. He wanted to own her. He wanted her to fear him just a little. Or maybe a lot. He wasn't sure how much of this was anger at her father and how much of it was what she did to him of her own accord . . . that sweet, bright, white innocence that clung to her, the scent of purity that wafted through the air like a meadow of lavender.

And he didn't care. She wasn't going anywhere. He didn't have to be soft with her. She had to adapt to him, not the other way around. Perhaps things could have been different if she hadn't been withheld and hidden from him for so long.

For thousands of years, he'd been bitter that Zeus and Poseidon got all the good stuff, and he'd drawn the short straw for the underworld. If he couldn't have the sky and the sea, he would have Persephone. And he had every intention of tormenting Zeus over it. He would drive her father mad if it was the last thing he did.

Even if he didn't send dear old daddy a package, Zeus would know plenty. It was the blessing and curse of being a god.

"My Lord?"

Hades felt the glow coming to his eyes. The guard was still standing there? "What?"

"Would it hurt you to show her a little mercy?"

Maybe. He didn't know if he wanted her to hate and fear him or if he wanted her to love him so he could rip the rug out from under her and watch as that love turned to shock and betrayal, then hatred and fear. The more he hurt her, the more it would destroy Zeus. And he liked that plan quite a lot.

"My Lord? This isn't her fault."

"Go back to your post."

The guard went back to his post along the long hall.

Of course it wasn't her fault. She was just a pawn in all this, but it was Zeus who had made the first move, and it was Hades who was going to finish it.

But the guard was right about one thing. Why should he keep her down in the dank dungeon by herself? He wanted to play with her, and his room was so much more comfortable. He could strike as much terror on the third floor as he could in the dungeon.

When he reached the bottom of the stairs, Persephone sat up and scooted to one corner of her cage. He was going to lock a collar around that tiny throat. And very soon.

She shivered as he approached, her clothes still wet from her earlier spill into the black sea. He unlocked the cage and opened the door. "Come with me."

She struggled to her feet and used the bars of the cage to steady herself as she made her way to him. When she'd stepped outside the cage, he was about to turn to go up the stairs, knowing she would follow, but before he could do that, she swayed on her feet.

Hades caught her just as she fainted. He wasn't sure if it was the cold, fear, or general exhaustion. Perhaps hunger. It wasn't as though a few pomegranate seeds would sustain her.

He carried her up the stairs to the main level, then up a grand staircase she no doubt would have been impressed by had she been conscious to see it, then up another level to his private floor.

Once in his room, he laid her down on the bed a bit more gently than he'd intended. He needed to get her out of these wet clothes. Hades absently waved a hand in the direction of a large fireplace near the bed. It immediately came to life with flames.

She flopped around like a rag doll while he removed her wet clothes. The T-shirt clung to her and peeled off as if she'd been shrink-wrapped in it. Next, he took her shoes—some ridiculous pair of aquamarine colored wedge sandals. Then the jeans. Panties. Bra.

He tossed the clothes in the fire then he stood over the bed and just looked at her. So perfect and fair and sweet. Did he really want to mar that perfect pale skin? Yes. He did. Anything he did to her would heal. Well, anything physical. She might not recover from the emotional scars.

Hades sat next to her on the bed. He leaned closer, his nose pressed against the side of her throat, breathing in that clean scent. He pulled back suddenly and just stared.

No. It wasn't possible. Was it? But how?

Hades held his hands a few inches above her and moved along the length of her body. He could sense and feel the nuances of her energy this way. When he was certain, he pulled away.

However improbable, Zeus had kept her sheltered in more than one way. Hades was absolutely sure. Persephone was a virgin. A sweet, innocent virgin, trapped in his underworld lair.

Instead of sending Zeus a finger, Hades thought maybe he should send a nice thank you card.

The sounds of the fire crackling and spitting in the grate woke Persephone. She felt weak and tired from hunger and fear. She hadn't even been blessed with a moment of the comfort of not remembering where she was. She wasn't in the cage at least.

No, instead, she was in a large comfortable bed, covered by a heavy black blanket, her head cushioned by three soft pillows. On one side of her was the fireplace and on the other was a large, open arched doorway covered only by wisps of sheer, black fabric. The fabric whispered whenever a soft breeze blew by.

Through the sheer material, Persephone could see a large stone balcony with some furniture as well as the sky and the bright full moon and stars. She was about to get up and go explore the balcony when she realized she was naked, and there was no clothing anywhere within her line of sight.

The door on the other end of the room opened, and Hades stepped in. She could smell the delicious aroma of food coming off the silver tray. He placed the tray next to her on the bed and sat on the edge beside her.

"Eat," he said. This time he sounded less crazy when he said that word.

She hesitated. She was so hungry, but then she remembered the pomegranate.

"You can only be tied eternally to me once. So you may as well eat something," he said, guessing correctly the cause of her hesitation.

The food on the tray was far more tempting than the fruit had been down in the dungeon: a small roasted chicken with herb and garlic mashed potatoes covered in butter and green beans that looked like they'd come straight from a garden to her plate without canning or freezing in between. A crystal goblet of water sat next to the plate.

"Where did it all come from?"

"Where does anything here come from? It's magic. But the food is real enough, and it will sustain you. Without your powers, you'll need to eat more frequently."

He was still on this goddess delusion.

"I'm twenty-five," she said. Not immortal. Not thousands of years old. Not whatever he thought she was.

"No. You think you're twenty-five," Hades said. "Eat before I lose my patience."

Not wanting to see that scary red glow that he could get in his eyes, Persephone ate. The food was as incredible as it looked. At least she probably wouldn't starve down here.

"Hades?" she said when she was almost finished. She already felt a little stronger. Strong enough maybe to ask the question that had been burning through her brain for a while now.

"Hmmm?"

He was still too uncomfortably close, sitting only inches away.

"What are you going to do with me?"

"I'm still deciding," he said.

"B-but you're still not going to kill me?"

"I told you, you can't be killed. You're immortal."

She was very sure she wasn't. Then, remembering her nudity, a more upsetting thought occurred to her. "Did you . . ."

A dark and devious smile lit his face. "Did I . . . what?"

"Well, I . . .I'm naked. Did you . . .?"

"Did I penetrate that sweet innocent little body? No. I want you conscious for that."

So he planned to. At some point.

Persephone swallowed hard around the last bite of chicken. Somehow it was less delicious than the previous bites, and it took a long drink of water to help get it down.

He took the tray away and set it on a small table near the door. When he returned to her bedside he said, "I know you can't tell me because you can't remember, but I would be fascinated to know how your father has kept you pure for thousands of years. That's . . . dedication. I can't imagine how it would even be possible."

Persephone had given up on trying to convince him she was just a human. It seemed a waste of the precious little energy she had.

"Okay, how about this?" Hades said. "How about you tell me how you've made it to twenty-five without a sexual part-ner. You've had opportunities. There is no way you haven't. You're far too beautiful to have been passed over."

She blushed at that even though she didn't want his words to have any effect at all.

"I don't know. I just wasn't really interested in dating."

He looked perplexed for a long while, then all at once, a dawning realization came over Hades' face. "He took your desire away. It wasn't enough to take your powers. He took everything that made you you, all so I wouldn't find you and take you."

Persephone wasn't sure if that was true. No, she was absolutely sure it wasn't because all of this was insane. She did appreciate male beauty. Even though she'd been afraid, she'd noticed that aesthetically Hades was just about perfect. But he was right; she couldn't remember ever reacting to a man in the way other girls around her had claimed to. She just . . . hadn't been interested in pursuing it. And a part of her felt that other women were . . . faking it somehow.

Maybe they just wanted to be liked or wanted, so they pretended to feel the same animal lust men directed at them.

"Well," Hades said, "I take this as a personal challenge. He can't keep you from me. His tricks might work with mortal men, but they won't stop you from reacting to me."

He reached out to stroke her cheek, and she flinched. Before he could react, there was a knock on the door.

"What is it?" he growled, not taking his eyes from her.

The door eased open a few inches at a time, and then a guard, looking far more timid than seemed natural for his terrifying stature, stepped into the room.

"I'm sorry to disturb you, My Lord. But there is a matter that needs your attention in the Eastern Sector."

Hades finally turned to the intruder, allowing her relief from that dark, assessing stare.

"It can't wait?"

"I'm afraid not, My Lord." The guard left and shut the door quietly behind him.

Hades went to the closet and pulled out a long, black velvet robe and laid it across the bed. "You can wear this while I'm away. I won't be gone long."

When he'd left, Persephone let out a long, tremulous breath. Gingerly, she got out of the bed and slipped into the robe. She hadn't expected it to fit so perfectly, or to look like a dress on her.

The inner lining was satin. The outside was a velvet brocade with intricate, subtle designs in the material. There were three silver clasps in the front. One at her breasts, one at her belly, and one several inches below her hips. When she walked, the fabric parted, to reveal perhaps a bit more thigh than she would have liked.

Practically everything she'd seen so far of the under-world and his castle made her feel as though she were trapped in a black and white movie. All the colors were muted. Nearly everything was black or silver. She didn't like the idea of wearing something that would make her seem more a part of this dismal, lonely world.

Persephone would have loved nothing more than to have found the clothes she'd arrived in, but either he'd hidden them or destroyed them. The doorknob clicked softly in her hand, and the momentary fear that he might have locked her in disappeared as she pushed the door open.

But when she stepped out into the hallway, it became immediately clear why he hadn't bothered locking it. A guard stood just outside.

Instead of flinging her back into the room and growling threats at her as she expected, he bowed and said, "Is there anything I can get you, Your Grace?"

"I-I'm sorry what?"

"Or My Queen. How do you prefer to be addressed?"

"There must be some mistake. I'm not the queen. I-I'm his prisoner."

"The prophecy was very clear. He's searched for you for nine centuries. He'd almost given up hope of finding you. You are the queen."

Funny, there had been no ceremony. No wedding. No coronation. She considered arguing with him some more, but if he thought she was his queen, it might be easier to get out of here. After all, prisoners couldn't exactly give orders and be taken seriously.

Persephone steadied herself. She would have to fight not to stutter. Even if she was afraid, and even if she wasn't really the queen of anything, the guard feared Hades and was unlikely to disrespect him by harming her in the god's absence. But she had to sell it.

"I would like to go outside the castle."

"Certainly, Your Grace. I can have a horse brought around for you. Would you like an escort to explore the kingdom?"

"No, I'll be fine on my own."

"Very well." He went ahead of her down the hall and down the stairs.

She hadn't really expected that to work and had to mask her shock when it did.

Persephone moved more slowly than the guard. It wouldn't do for her to rush or run. They might become suspicious about her intentions. In reality, she had no clue how she was going to get out of here, but she couldn't just sit around and wait for the crazy guy who had already threatened to cut off her finger to return. This might be her only opportunity.

She was halfway down the hall before she realized she had no shoes. Would it be dangerous to leave the castle without shoes? The guard hadn't seemed to think so, if he'd even noticed at all.

She went down one flight of stairs, and then there was another more grand and elaborate staircase of black marble. This staircase led down to the long entry hall she remembered before he'd dragged her down to the dungeon and thrown her in a cage.

The guards lining the walls down on the main level didn't spare her a glance or try to stop her. Outside there was a black horse waiting for her. She wasn't sure if it was the horse she'd had from before. The guard from outside her room stood next to it.

"Could you get me some shoes, please?" she asked, trying not to sound too pleading. If he thought she was the queen, pleading might give away the truth.

"I'm afraid Hades left no shoes for you. But don't worry. There is nothing here in the underworld that would dare harm you."

If those things knew she was trying to escape they might.

The guard helped her up into the saddle. His eyes glowed red, and his nostrils flared at the glimpse he got between her legs. She'd forgotten all she was wearing was a robe. She pulled the velvet over her and urged the horse away from the castle.

Each time the horse moved, the smooth leather saddle rubbed between her legs, eliciting a sensation that was altogether foreign and frightening in its strangeness. If only she could have found her other clothes. Anything to put a barrier between her naked skin and soft leather moving at a fierce, rhythmic pace against her.

She fought to ignore it as she guided the horse through the vast, dead meadow and to the mouth of the dead, black forest. She dug her heel into the horse's side and he started to race through the tangled woods. He moved so fast, she had to lean forward to keep from falling, and she quickly forgot the disturbing sensations of only moments before.

When they got through the forest, she dismounted and tied the horse up to a tree. She couldn't just let him wander back home without her. Then she walked through the long dark tunnel. When she reached the gate, she saw that the giant three-headed dog was sleeping.

Persephone couldn't have hoped for greater luck. She eased past him and pushed the gate open. She winced as it creaked. But the dog snored on.

She'd only gotten one foot outside the gate when a giant paw pulled her back inside. Cerberus growled at her. Hades' warning that the dog might try to eat her face if she attempted escape came flooding back all of a sudden, and she started to cry.

All three mouths on the dog started to whimper. One of the heads bent down to . . . nuzzle her? At least the beast wasn't going to kill her. Or at least it didn't appear that he would. Suddenly she felt so unbelievably tired.

Not only could Persephone not face the defeat of returning to the castle of her own accord, she felt too exhausted to move. Cerberus might not be prepared to let her escape the underworld, but the dog had settled back down to nap again. He curled up and laid his giant heads down. Persephone curled up next to the dog and fell asleep in his soft fur.

Three

Hades was enraged that she would try to flee him. At the same time, seeing her snuggled up with Cerberus took the worst of the angry edge off. Of course she'd try to get away—at least until she realized how futile it was. The guards had known but hadn't attempted to stop her. They all knew the dog would. And the farther she was allowed to get before the trap shut, the more quickly she would come to understand her predicament.

The sooner she accepted things, the better for her.

She stirred when he picked her up. "Hades?"

He didn't reply. He simply waited for her to finish waking up, and then he helped her onto his horse. Hers had become untethered and gone back to the castle on its own. Hades climbed on the horse behind her and urged the mare toward home.

Tension radiated off her, but he didn't seek to ease it. They were both silent during the ride through the forest and the meadow. He spent most of the trip thinking about the business in the Eastern Sector, mostly to keep his mind off the slim warm body pressed against his own.

The problem could have been handled by someone else. It was a minor dispute between some of the beings that lived there, extremely boring. He could have left someone else to handle it and come back sooner, but he'd wanted to know what Persephone would do in his absence. And now he had his answer, though he couldn't blame her. He'd try to escape this place, too.

When they reached the castle, Hades helped her down from the horse and handed the reins to the groom to take care of, then he led her back inside the stone walls and up to his room.

He left her and went out onto the balcony to think. He looked out over the edge. It was a huge and deadly drop-off into an abyss with jagged stalagmites waiting to rip open any fool who fell down there. Or it would be if anyone mortal and alive were to fall.

Hades looked up at the sky then, at the moon and stars all maintained by magic. It was beautiful, but it was a dark and dreary sort of beauty. He couldn't help wishing that he could enjoy the sunlight just once. Persephone felt like the closest he would ever get to sunlight, the closest he could ever get to life itself.

He heard her tentative footsteps on the stone floor of the balcony. "Sit," he said, forcing the hardness back into his voice. He didn't turn until he heard her sit on one of the plush black loungers. Hades pulled up a chair and joined her. He looked at her for a long while. For once, he wasn't bothered that so much in his world was black.

The robe made her skin look luminescent in the moonlight. And that hair. He wanted to reach out and run his fingers through that hair.

Instead, he crossed his arms over his chest. "Where exactly did you think you were going today, Persephone?"

She looked down at her hands and shrugged.

"Really? You insult me with lies on top of everything else? Tell me the truth."

"I wanted to go back home."

"You are home."

She flinched at that.

"I'm afraid I'll have to punish you for trying to escape."

"Are you going to chop off a finger?"

She sounded more bitter than afraid, and he found himself unexpectedly relieved by it. He wanted to punish her. He wanted to turn her into a dark thing like him, something that craved all the things he did. But she seemed so fragile, so breakable. And some part of him couldn't seem to remember that he was supposed to be getting even with Zeus and that he shouldn't be soft with her.

"Nothing so grim as that," he said. But he could tell from the look on her face that she didn't believe him. That was probably wise. From minute to minute he couldn't decide what he wanted to do with her—what he was prepared to do with her.

Hades withdrew a large slim box from his coat, it was the one thing he knew for sure.

"What's this?" she asked when he gave it to her.

"A finger."

She dropped the box. "What?"

Hades chuckled. "I'm fucking with you. It's a collar. For you." He picked it up and opened it to show her there were no body parts inside. She didn't seem much more enthused by the box's actual contents.

"A collar?" she said uncertainly as she looked at the smooth silver band of metal cushioned inside the box. "I don't understand."

Was she that naive or only playing at it?

If Zeus hadn't kept her from him, Hades wondered if he would have given her a crown instead. It would have been a more appropriate piece of jewelry for a queen, but all he'd been able to think about for hundreds of years was possessing her. And over time that desire for possession had turned to an irrational need for absolute ownership.

He didn't want some sweet delicate thing that he would pamper and shield from his darkness. He wanted his lovely goddess on her knees.

"So I'm to be your slave."

She did understand. Good.

Hades removed the collar from the box, unlatched it, and locked it around her throat.

Quiet tears moved down her cheeks, but she managed to speak without the tears reaching her voice. "You should talk to your people. They think I'm the queen."

She shivered as Hades ran his fingers through her hair. He knew she would be unable to resist now that he was so close to her.

"You are the queen to them. And they better treat you like it. If I find out anyone has shown you even the smallest disrespect, they will pay dearly."

Persephone seemed confused by this, but why should she be confused? Couldn't she be his slave and their queen? Hades didn't see the complication. It made perfect sense to him.

"Will I ever see my family again? Or friends? Or Lynette?"

She was being remarkably brave. For as fragile as she looked, it was as though there was a strong core of steel inside her.

"You can never go back."

Her bravery faded almost as quickly as it had come on, and she began to sob in earnest. Hades fought against the urge to comfort her. There were places inside him, places frozen for centuries that this tiny creature could melt if he allowed her to get too close.

She made him feel somehow powerless, and it was that feeling that strengthened his resolve. He would punish her. He would rule her. And she would submit sweetly to his every desire. Or else. He could never let anyone in who had the power to hurt him.

You couldn't trust people. Mortal or god. They would all find a way to take things from you. He'd learned that the hard way with Zeus and Poseidon.

He couldn't allow Persephone to become too much to him. He would enjoy her but keep her at a distance. He would break her just enough so that he could manage her— so she couldn't manage him.

"Come," he said. "It's time for your punishment."

"H-Hades . . . please. I won't run again."

"Master."

"What?"

"You will call me Master."

If she kept calling him by his name he was going to crumble and give her anything she wanted. And no daughter of Zeus could ever be trusted. Despite knowing she was an innocent in all this, Hades couldn't help but feel the apple couldn't fall very far from the tree. Underneath this sweet delicate exterior there must be something disloyal. He would never give her the chance to unleash it.

"Persephone?" he prodded.

She looked up, her bright blue eyes made somehow brighter by her tears. "Yes, Master?" she whispered.

There was a mixture of satisfaction along with a tiny hard ball of pain inside him at hearing the helpless defeat in her voice. He could get drunk on that strange blend.

He held out a hand. "Come."

She didn't argue or beg him again. She just put her hand inside his and allowed him to lead her back inside. He took her out of the room and down the hallway to a separate large room he kept for play.

There were souls down here who had arrived in the underworld so broken, so in need of punishment, that he'd brought them into this room to give them what it was that they so desperately seemed to need. They were the lost souls —not quite bad enough to be sent to the lower realms, but not good enough to find any peace. It was mercy he offered them, a kind of absolution. And in those moments, he had been able to pretend he wasn't so utterly and completely alone.

Each of them had been resigned to her fate, whimpering sweetly under each implement of pain he wielded. When he was finished with each of them, they were able to move on to a better place in the underworld, having worked through their various issues and paid for their various misdeeds.

But Persephone was something entirely different.

She seemed far too innocent to deserve punishment for anything—even for running from him. Seeking freedom was hardly an unforgivable act. He could relate. He sometimes wanted it just as badly as she did.

Hades kept the playroom bare when it wasn't in use. All furniture, toys, and whipping implements stayed inside large closets, leaving the room one large open stone square. An enormous window on the south side of the room allowed the moonlight to shine in. He waved a hand and warm flames lit the torches along the wall.

He guided her to the center of the room and unlatched the three silver clasps of the robe. She didn't protest or fight him when he pushed it off her shoulders. He would give almost anything to know what she was thinking.

He folded it and laid the thick soft fabric on the ground. "Kneel on the robe. You can lay your head down."

As if locked in a trance, she did what he asked. He crossed to the closet and took out a riding crop. When he returned to her, she was crying quietly, her small body trembling on the robe she knelt on.

"You've never been physically punished for anything have you?"

She shook her head. "No, Master."

He'd expected more fight from her, more resistance. But she must know it would only make things worse. The hopelessness of her situation must have settled in.

"Is that because you never deserved to be punished or because those with authority over you were too soft?"

"I don't know."

Even if she had been punished for something, it wouldn't have been like this, with her nude. He couldn't pretend this wasn't sexual for him—as it would be for her once she understood what had been taken from her just to keep her pure and hidden.

"There was nowhere they could have hidden you from me that I wouldn't have eventually uncovered. Fate doesn't work that way."

She took a deep shuddering breath, and when it spilled out of her, Hades let the riding crop fall against her flesh. She gasped, as if shocked, but she didn't cry or beg or speak at all.

Maybe she was only trying to appease the man she no doubt still believed was crazy.

Her pale skin reacted immediately to the bite of the crop, turning a lovely pink in the spot where he'd struck her. He wanted to run his tongue over its warmth and soothe the sting, but he wasn't done yet.

Hades made a row of pretty pink welts across her back. She flinched each time the crop sliced through the air. Each time it landed, he was rewarded with a new sound from her. A gasp, then a whimper, then a mewl. He wondered if he could teach and train her so that it turned into a moan.

There were seven marks on her otherwise perfect skin. And now he knew. Not only did she need to eat like a human, she healed like a human. He was still reasonably certain her finger would have grown back eventually without her powers, but he was glad he wouldn't have to find out.

"Master, p-please," she said.

Ordinarily he wouldn't allow begging to stop him. He couldn't allow that manipulation. But she wasn't manipulating him. It was a sincere plea from someone who had bravely accepted her punishment.

He put the riding crop on the ground and sat beside her on the cold stone. There were far worse things he could have done, but he wanted to ease her into his world slowly. For as much as he wanted to use her to get back at her father, there was a piece of him that knew once his anger was sated, she'd still be here. And he needed her to be a whole being and not look on him with utter contempt and hatred.

He might be afraid to let her in, but he still had to protect her to some degree. She'd been meant for him from the start. How could he break his toy in a fit of childish rage? He couldn't. He had to be careful with her.

Persephone had thought once Hades started he might never stop. He didn't always seem altogether sane or present. She tried to be brave, hoping it would appease him, but the uncertainty of how far he might take things . . . She hadn't wanted to play on his mercy—or the small bits of it she'd seen so far. Begging had worked to stop him from cutting off her finger. And now it had worked to stop the strip of leather he'd struck her with.

But for how long would it work?

She was afraid to overplay her hand, afraid he might work past whatever ambivalence he felt about hurting her. It was beginning to dawn on her that she was going to have to find a way to exist with this man in this awful underground place where the sky was just another lie—and not even a comforting one.

She couldn't convince herself that things would be better in the morning. There was no morning—no dawn to soften the edges of the fears that creep in at night. Somehow, she was sure the darkness was the worst of it.

When Hades sat next to her on the ground and pulled her into his arms, she didn't resist him. It was the first moment of real tenderness he'd shown her. She couldn't even argue with herself about this. She didn't want to resist or fight. This place just by virtue of its absolute crushing darkness was too exhausting all by itself. She had to have an ally here. Even if it was her captor.

Escape was impossible. Since that was the case, all she could do was figure out how to make her existence here more tolerable. He seemed content for the others to see and treat her as the queen. That meant there was only one being down here she had to fear, so it seemed smart to her to get him on her side as quickly as possible, before he changed his mind about how the other beings here were to treat her.

She jumped in his arms when his tongue moved over the welts he'd left on her. She couldn't see them, but she could feel them. Each of them had been a sharp, penetrating sting at first and then a strip of bright hot warmth that felt like the only warmth in the underworld.

His tongue was followed by lips, pressing soft kisses, then fingers stroking along her back.

He'd made some of his intentions with her clear already. When he took her, would he be gentle like this. Would it be in his bed? Would he give her the illusion of romance? Somehow, she doubted it with the way he talked about hurting Zeus. And he was still convinced she was this goddess of spring he'd been looking for.

The only hope Persephone now held of getting out of this place was that Hades would realize she was just a normal mortal and release her—if he didn't feel she'd somehow tricked him.

The longer he held her the more it felt as though inside the circle of his arms was where she was meant to be. She wanted to fight that thought, but fighting was so exhausting. Even the idea of it made her want to sleep for a thousand years. She wanted to make this easy on herself.

And the way Hades was touching her right now made it so easy to want to get lost inside him, to pretend he was a man who could love and care for her and that this place wasn't so bad.

"Master?"

"Hmmm?"

Would her petty human needs begin to annoy him? "I'm hungry."

It didn't seem like it was possible, but it had been hours since she'd last eaten. She couldn't be sure with no sun to mark time and guide her but she felt as though she'd slept for a very long time with Cerberus. She must have for Hades to have been away dealing with whatever business he'd had before he'd come for her and brought her back to the castle.

And how long had they been here in this room? It felt like forever.

"Come downstairs to the dining hall when you're ready. I'll have something good for you." He got up off the ground and left her alone.

When he'd left, it was like a fog of cold sadness swept over and around her. She felt so tired and sad all of a sudden.

Persephone wasn't leaving a big exciting life behind. But it had been warm and safe and comforting. She'd loved everything about it. She'd had a small studio apartment over a Chinese restaurant a couple of blocks from the flower shop.

It was on a corner with a park right across the street. Because of this location, her apartment got a surprising amount of sunlight for being in such a big city with so many buildings everywhere fighting to crowd out the light.

The rent had been low, they said, because of all the cooking smells she'd have to deal with. But she loved it. She'd filled the place up with plants that seemed to like the smell of the food as much as she did.

The couple that owned the restaurant ran a special on lo mein and egg rolls on Wednesdays, and the old Chinese woman always overcooked that day. She always brought leftovers upstairs to Persephone along with a handful of fortune cookies.

"Open the right one, you might find a husband," she'd teased each week.

They both knew a fortune cookie couldn't do that, and Persephone hadn't had the heart to tell the old woman that she didn't think a husband was in her future. It didn't feel like anybody else in the world fit her.

Even in a city so big, she'd never felt that excited swept-away feeling she thought she was supposed to feel. She'd admired her fair share of male models and actors and construction workers as they'd drifted past the door of the flower shop, but it had never been more than a passing aesthetic admiration.

She'd never felt the wild urge to try to flirt or get to know one of them or to do something more carnal.

She hadn't spoken to her dad in a couple of years, not since her mom died. They'd had a fight. They'd said some things. And they'd both been too stubborn to apologize and make it right. She'd run off to New York and left him with the farm. She knew her dad needed her—at least to talk to her. And now more than ever she wished she'd made things right while she'd had the chance.

The only good thing was that he wouldn't know she was missing. Knowing that would probably kill him, especially with mom already gone.

In the city she'd made a few friends, mostly regulars that hung out at the Chinese restaurant below her apartment. Then there was the shopkeeper at the bookstore across from her job she'd formed a friendship with. And Lynette at the flower shop.

It was such a small life tucked inside a couple of blocks of an enormous city. But she'd been content. And now those plants were all going to die. Her apartment would be rented.

Her job would be filled. And she could kiss free Chinese food on Wednesdays goodbye.

She wasn't sure how long she'd stayed on the ground thinking about this, mourning the finality and the loss of everything and everyone she loved. Even if it hadn't been a big life, it had been her life. She'd been so happy she'd never stopped to consider how unhappy she could be if it were all taken.

Now she knew.

And it wasn't the fear of what he might do to her. Surprisingly the closest thing she'd felt down here to the happiness of her life up there had been when Hades was holding her. She didn't want to think too hard about that, and she definitely couldn't bring herself to fight it. She had to find a way to hold onto this one warm thing even if he was also the source of all her problems.

Persephone got up off the ground and put the robe back on, carefully locking the three silver clasps back in place. In the hallway, she found another guard. This time she was less afraid, though she did worry he might have heard what Hades had done in there with her.

She felt the marks the god had left on her as they pressed against the soft fabric of the robe. She was so very aware of that—and her nudity. Strangely, after the whipping, she was more aware of her nudity under the robe, of how the slit in the garment rested mere inches south of a place between her legs that felt suddenly awake.

Her nipples were aroused and pressing against the fabric. It was such a foreign sensation. She hoped the guard didn't notice. She'd never been more aware of her own body before in her life. Something dark and carnal felt as though it were slithering between her legs, then up and around her belly, over her breasts, pulling her into a mad embrace she didn't think she could survive and couldn't decide if she wanted, even though a craving had started that very much was not for food.

"Your Grace," the guard said.

It was still weird being called that.

"My Lord Hades said I should wait for you and help you find the dining hall."

"O-okay. Thank you," Persephone managed as she tried desperately to stop thinking all the thoughts that had insisted on pushing into her mind at just the wrong and most mortifying moment.

She followed the guard downstairs and down several massive hallways until they reached a large room that contained a long, shiny, black table. The guard excused himself back to his duties, and Persephone stepped inside. There was a long row of tall windows where the moonlight cast reflections on the table.

Hades had set a fire roaring in the grate of an enormous fireplace on one wall. He pulled out a chair for her at the end of the table near the fire as if he knew how much she needed to feel something warm and bright on her skin—the smallest echo of sunlight.

He waved a hand, and several silver candelabras with white candles lit all down the length of the table. Instead of leaving her alone and sitting all the way at the other end, he pulled a chair up beside her.

"Eat," he said.

She looked down at a shiny black plate in front of her. It was empty. But then a second later it was filled with lo mein and egg rolls. Exactly like from the Chinese restaurant.

"An interesting choice," Hades remarked.

"H-how?"

"The castle knows what you want," he said.

Then the castle must know how badly she wanted to return to her life on the surface. If the castle could magically deliver the food she'd just been thinking of, couldn't it take her back to her life?

A silver goblet beside the plate filled with water as if it were being poured from an unseen pitcher.

Persephone didn't give voice to her thoughts of escape. Even if the castle could know her deepest desire to return to her life, it would never defy Hades to deliver her that one fervent wish. She was sure that the castle, like the guards, were loyal to him.

Instead, she ate as requested. It was exactly like the food she remembered, down to the strange touch of cinnamon inside the egg rolls that made all the other flavors pop. Hades sat quietly beside her while she ate. It was unnerving, but it was better than eating alone.

"Don't you eat?" she asked.

"I do, but I don't need to nearly as often as you."

When she'd finished, the plate cleared away and became clean and shiny again. A moment later, a single fortune cookie appeared.

Persephone opened it and read the small slip of paper inside.

Give the dark mysterious man a chance. He's not all bad.

"Did you do this?" she asked, passing the fortune to Hades.

He read the slip of paper and chuckled. "No. The castle has a weird sense of humor sometimes."

"What now?" Persephone asked.

One dark eyebrow rose. "What do you mean, what now?"

"I mean what happens now? What are you going to do to me now?"

Hades pulled back his sleeve and looked at a gleaming silver watch on his wrist. "It's midnight in the city you came from. You should get some rest. And then in a few days, we'll throw a party. I can't hide you away from the whole under-world now can I?"

"How will I ever know what day it is?"

Hades covered her hand with his and closed his eyes for a moment. When he opened them, the watch had somehow transferred from his wrist to hers. She'd been so busy watch-ing him, that she hadn't seen the magic happen.

"I'll have another made for myself," he said.

"T-thank you." Was there a possibility he might be kind to her? Couldn't he forget this vendetta against Zeus and be decent?

She looked down at the watch. In the transfer from his wrist to hers, it had also gotten smaller—not just to fit her much tinier wrist, but the band had gotten slimmer to give it a more feminine feel. The face of the watch was a normal time piece, but right above the face where the band started there was a little moon symbol.

"The watch is set for New York time. When it's day, that moon will change to a sun," Hades said as she studied it.

Under the face of the watch, where the other band started, there was a date and a year so she would know what day it was, too. Even though this place seemed like a stag-nant endless noise of no time, the watch around her wrist felt like the smallest window back into the real world. At least she could know how many days, weeks, months had passed. She could know if the sun was out in her world, or if it was night.

She could know when to sleep and get up, assuming Hades allowed her to keep to some kind of normal schedule. He seemed like he might. Since her punishment, something in him seemed to have unwound the smallest amount as if some darkness inside him had been appeased, allowing her a small window of safety. And in that window, he wanted her to sleep.

"Go on up to bed, Sunshine," he said.

She felt his eyes on her as she got up from the table. Then it was the eyes of the guards she felt as she walked down the hallways, up the grand staircase, and up to the third floor and the room with the big, comfortable bed.

Inside the room was a big black door she hadn't noticed before. When she pushed it open, she found a clean, simple bathroom. When she glanced at the marble counter, a toothbrush and toothpaste appeared along with a fluffy gray towel.

She took the watch off and laid it on the counter, along with the robe he'd dressed her in. The silver collar gleamed at her throat. She didn't know how to take it off or even if she was allowed to, so she left it on. Then she took a hot shower and brushed her teeth.

Admittedly, a good meal and the normalcy of a shower and a toothbrush made her feel somehow less stricken by everything.

She wrapped the gray towel around herself and put the watch back on. Persephone didn't bother with the robe. If Hades wanted her, he would have her, and no flimsy piece of fabric would get in his way. She would rather at least be comfortable under the soft sheets and blanket.

She got into the bed and dropped the towel onto the floor, where it promptly vanished into thin air.

Four

Persephone stirred, awakened by a warm body pressing against hers. "It's only me, Sunshine," Hades said. Only him. Only her tormentor. Only the end of the world.

But when his skin was pressed against hers, she didn't feel any of the things she thought she was supposed to feel. When he was touching her, she wasn't afraid. She didn't feel cold or unhappy. Everything felt warm and safe. She didn't want him to ever stop touching her because as long as his skin was pressed against hers everything in her world felt right somehow.

"Master are you going to . . .?"

"Am I going to what?"

"You know what." She couldn't bring herself to say it. She knew he had every intention of . . . deflowering her. And yet, with his warmth edging so close into hers, she couldn't think of why that should be a bad thing. It seemed as though she had always been meant for him and that he had always been meant for her. And despite everything that should make that idea wrong, it felt right.

Still, she looked at him expectantly, hoping he wouldn't make her say the words.

Hades sighed. "Fine. Yes, I know what you're asking. But no, not just yet. You need rest. I'll start training you tomorrow and then . . . we'll see. When your desire is so great you can't cope with life without me inside you, and when you then beg me to fulfill that lust, I'll let you have it."

She tried to ignore most of that, though the words had tunneled into her brain and would likely stay there forever to taunt her. "Training?" she asked, trying instead to focus on one small part of his troubling speech.

"Oh, yes, Sunshine. I have to awaken you. You are not a little girl. You are a woman with needs you will become aware of very soon. If you were fated to be mine, then the needs inside you must mirror mine as well. They've just been buried. But for now . . . sleep."

Persephone was sure she'd only closed her eyes for a moment, but the watch around her wrist showed a little sun with the time reading nine thirty. She'd slept like the dead. Then remembering where she was, that seemed suddenly very logical.

She tried to think what had woken her because it certainly wasn't sunlight. Then she heard the steady patter of water in Hades' bathroom and realized the sound of the shower must have been what pulled her out of sleep. If he had taken Lynette instead of Persephone, she was sure her boss would be seducing him in the shower right now.

Lynette wouldn't have been as afraid. Despite seeming to share the quiet life of the flower shop, Lynette liked to party, and she liked dangerous men. She was the kind of woman dangerous men liked as well. Her back and left arm were covered in black tattoos, though her long hair usually covered most of it. Sometimes she wore a cropped top to give a peak of a dragon climbing out of the back of red leather pants.

Lynette would have barely reached the underworld before she'd have herself convinced she'd gone there of her own free will. She certainly wouldn't have kicked up a fuss and fought. It wouldn't have occurred to her to be afraid of a man as utterly visually beautiful as Hades. She would have counted herself lucky and ridden him into oblivion.

But Persephone wasn't Lynette. She didn't know how to play the temptress. And even if she did, she would only be pretending. She might feel inexplicably warm and safe when Hades touched her, but she didn't feel the animal craving of lust. She didn't know what it was to *need* a man inside her.

A few minutes later, the shower stopped. And then several minutes after that, Hades came out wearing jeans and a black T-shirt. No shoes. Dripping hair. He almost looked human. He almost looked like one of those models that might drift past the flower shop window on a bright Thursday afternoon.

"Did you sleep well?"

She went suddenly shy. "Yes, Master."

When she looked up again, he was smiling softly at her. All at once, she felt as though her will had enfolded into his, and somehow she knew he wouldn't have gone for Lynette.

"Are you hungry?" he asked, still conversational, still so . . . normal.

"I'm not really much of a breakfast person. I don't usually eat until eleven thirty."

"Good. I have big plans for you today."

She wasn't sure when it had happened, but there must have been a moment when Hades had decided keeping her in a cage and chopping off fingers was no longer appealing. Because even though she knew the reality of her situation, increasingly it felt as though he saw her as something other than his prisoner, and for small moments at a time, she found she could fall into that version of reality as well.

He crossed the room to the side of the bed and held out a hand. "Come with me."

Suddenly she was very aware of her nudity. "C-can I have the robe?"

A smirk inched up one side of his face. "No, you may not."

"But there are guards out there."

"Believe me, they've seen thousands of beautiful naked women. You won't shock them."

She felt the heat rise to her cheeks. "But . . ."

"Persephone, in my world, we like our nudity. There is nothing for you to be ashamed or shy about."

His words didn't change the way she felt about it, but it was his world, and he knew how things worked down here. If Hades said nudity was no big deal, then maybe it wasn't. Either way, he was being so pleasant with her, and she found herself not wanting to disappoint him. She allowed him to help her out of the bed and lead her down the hall to the room he'd punished her in before.

They only passed one guard on the way, who was stationed outside the bedroom. And he only took one quick look before Hades had her safely behind the doors of his playroom away from curious eyes.

She felt so strange standing in the moonlight from the window. It should be sunny. Or at least light out. There should be birds chirping and some kind of weather. But instead, it was just that dead, shiny blackness and bright, full moon. The moon didn't even change. There were no phases . . . because it wasn't real.

When Hades touched her and made her feel warm and safe, was that just magic like the moon? Was it even real? Or was it only a bit of sorcery to keep her from fighting him?

"D-do you use magic on me?"

He frowned. "What do you mean use magic *on* you?"

"I mean . . . are you doing something to me when you touch me?"

"Nothing besides touching you," he said, an evil smirk lighting his face.

Persephone searched for a sign of deceit, but if it was there, it was too cleverly masked for her to find.

Hades waved a hand, and something that looked like a big leather table shot out from the closet and then hovered and settled in the center of the room. A pile of pillows landed on top of the table, and then a thick black blanket covered it all.

His attention shifted to her. "Get on top and make yourself comfortable."

She climbed onto the table while he stood a few feet away and watched. She wasn't sure what he meant by making herself comfortable. Should she lie down? Sit there? This felt so strange and awkward.

"Hmmm," Hades said. "One adjustment." He went to the closet and brought out a rounded, wide leather bench with a flat bottom. He pushed a few of the pillows aside and placed it in the middle of the table.

"Straddle it."

"I-I'm sorry what?" She already felt far too exposed on the table. No one had ever seen her naked like this. Nor had anyone ever requested she spread her legs. The idea would have been vulgar. Although she'd known in a vague sort of way about sex, she'd never stopped to think out any of the details or how it might play out against real living flesh.

He chuckled and moved to stand closer to the table. "Tell me the truth, Persephone. Don't you want to see all that's been hidden from you? Don't you want to understand it? Feel it? Taste it? Be consumed by it?" His voice was so low and hypnotic.

She thought about playing dumb, but she understood him perfectly. And maybe she did want to know. For years, she'd thought there was something very wrong with her. That something was broken. Why couldn't she feel the things other people around her felt? It was as though she'd been trapped in an earlier stage of development, and everyone else was leaving her behind to experience the more adult aspects of the world while she stayed in the safe family-friendly sphere of life.

She wanted to know if it was real or if they were only pretending. What if she could feel those same things? She thought back to her escape attempt and the feel of the leather saddle rubbing between her legs. That had been . . . new, and though a little scary, not entirely unwelcome.

Maybe there *was* something there that Hades could awaken. He seemed so worldly and experienced. If anyone knew all the carnal mysteries of the world, it was this guy. And a part of her, that kept growing louder by the moment, wanted him to reveal every secret to her.

"Sunshine, come on this trip with me. Let me teach you everything."

He didn't make threats or remind her of her captivity. He just waited patiently. There was no need for threats. The temptation was too dark, too delicious. He could drag her deeper down into his hedonistic world with only the promises of the pleasures she wanted to know.

Finally, she did as he asked. The leather was soft against her skin as she spread her legs over it, much as the saddle had been. She had to stop herself from grinding against it, trying to mimic that feeling from the day before.

Hades pulled out straps from underneath the table and secured her legs down. Then he took some rope from the closet and tied her wrists behind her back. She hadn't realized restraints would be involved.

"Are you afraid?"

She looked down at the table. "Yes, Master."

He pressed a hand against her cheek, and she immediately calmed and leaned into it, still convinced he was doing some magic thing when he touched her. She hadn't remembered feeling this way when he'd grabbed her as he'd taken her from the city.

If his touch had elicited this response back then, she never could have brought herself to fight him, no matter how much her rational mind might have screamed at her to.

"I'll be right back."

Hades left the room for a few minutes. If he had been gone any longer, she might have started to panic, but he returned well before she could start worrying about isolation and bondage.

And he brought company.

Persephone's eyes widened upon seeing two additional people led into the room—a man and a woman. It was one thing for a guard to catch a quick glance as she'd walked down the hall with Hades; it was another for her legs to be spread so wide and her hands tied behind her back thrusting her breasts forward for these two strangers to look at . . . or reach out and touch. She squeezed her eyes shut.

"Persephone," Hades said. "I want you to watch them."

The man and woman moved to the far end of the room. Both of them were naked and so utterly perfect. The woman was small, much like Persephone, with dark auburn hair that went halfway down her back. The man was tall and large with dark hair like Hades. He was all hard, solid planes of muscle against her slim yielding softness.

The woman got on her hands and knees on the floor, and the man moved in behind her. His erection was thick and ready. He looked far too large for the woman he was about to take pleasure in. And yet Persephone couldn't bring herself to look away as he impaled her, and the woman let out a sharp gasp.

At first it was merely fascinating, like watching a nature show.

Hades came closer to Persephone. His hand moved underneath her hair and trailed over the back of her neck, stroking small soothing circles. His voice was low when he spoke. "Watch the animal way he takes her. Watch the sweet way she submits to him and accepts each inch as he penetrates her."

There was no need for Hades to narrate, but the silky smoothness of his words caused a light throbbing to begin between Persephone's legs. Without at first realizing what she was doing, she started to move back and forth against the leather.

"She belongs to him, just like you belong to me. This is exactly how it should be," Hades whispered, his hand still stroking the back of Persephone's neck.

The woman moaned as the man began rubbing between her legs as he continued to fuck her from behind. After a few moments, the man let out a sound like a roar and came, gripping the woman's hips hard, leaving red marks that would later bruise.

He pulled out of her and flipped her hard onto her back. Her eyes were so glazed with lust that if it hurt, she wouldn't feel it for a while.

"Spread her legs wide for us," Hades said. "We want to see everything."

The man spread her open so that Persephone had a good clear view between the woman's thighs. She was wet, and her sex was swollen from the stimulation—like a flower blooming in the heat of a summer day.

Her hips moved as his fingers slid easily over the damp, swollen flesh. Persephone's hips moved as well, against the leather, wishing Hades, or even that man, was touching her like that. She wanted to feel what the woman was feeling. She wanted to completely give herself over to whatever this was.

Time held no meaning as she watched the woman on the ground being touched. The woman didn't seem to care that she was putting on a show for Persephone and Hades. All she cared about was her orgasm.

The man pressed his fingers harder against her, while the fingers of the other hand dipped inside her and began pumping like his cock had moments ago when she'd been on her knees. Just as then, she happily received every stroking sensation he offered her.

After a few moments, the build up exploded out of her, and she came bucking and screaming, arching up off the stone floor. Her whole body was flushed pink, and she trembled as she rode the wave of pleasure. Then she was still, and he was still, the two of them cuddled together on the ground.

"You may go," Hades said.

The man and woman didn't look like they were nearly done with each other, but they obeyed the god's command and left the room.

Hades turned to Persephone. "How do you feel?"

She felt warm, tingly, scared, excited. Like she needed to be touched. But all these thoughts came at her at once so that she couldn't pick one out or find a way to explain it even though the words had seemed ready inside her mind only moments before.

Her nipples felt tight and erect, and the leather had grown damp between her legs as her arousal had intensified.

"If I decided to fuck you right now, how would you feel?"

Her breath caught. Words didn't want to come out. The only thing that managed to make its way out of her throat was a small whimper.

"Are you ready to beg me for it like a good girl?"

She did feel something happening. Something strange and wonderful, but she wasn't quite ready to be that wanton yet. She didn't think she could beg him to take her.

"I didn't think so. No matter. I have plenty more to make that sweet little body ready for me."

Hades waved an arm and long white sheets fluttered down from the ceiling, closing her in on all sides like a fabric box. He remained on the other side where she could only see his shadow.

Moments later, images flashed on the fabric like a movie. There was a close-up of a naked man, his cock hard and ready. And then a woman on her knees in front of him open-ing her mouth to take his large erection between her lips. The other sheets of fabric had other similarly sexual images until all Persephone could see was a tangle of bodies rubbing and touching and sucking and fucking.

It wasn't just images. There was sound. Moaning. Heavy breathing. Begging. "Please, Master, harder. Your filthy little whore needs to come." Deep masculine chuckles of amuse-ment followed.

An intoxicating scent like cinnamon candy filled the air, and Persephone realized it was some sort of flavored body cream one of the men was using on a woman's nipples. He sucked them into his mouth as she writhed against him.

The orgy seemed to go on for hours. No one got tired or slowed down in their driving need to chase orgasm after orgasm. No amount of pleasure was ever enough for them to consider stopping. The smells and sounds and visuals were sending Persephone into a frenzy. The leather bench began to feel so slippery beneath her that if she weren't tied down, she might slide off.

She struggled in her bonds. The ropes chafed at her wrists. She'd rubbed and rubbed herself against the leather, but she needed more. She needed her hands free.

"Master, please!" She couldn't believe how loud and desperate her own voice had sounded.

The orgy stopped, and they all seemed to . . . look at her? Wasn't it just a video? Were they real? Could they see her? It hadn't occurred to her for one moment that they could see her as well as she could see them. And even if they could, they'd only been interested in fulfilling their own lusts with each other, unconcerned with any nearby voyeurs.

Before she could question the reality of what she'd seen any further, the images, smells, and sounds all disappeared. The fabric was suddenly just fabric, and it was pulled back up into the ceiling again, leaving only Hades standing in front of her, his eyes glowing with pure lust.

"Are you ready to be touched now?" he asked.

"Y-yes, Master."

"Beg me. Pleasure has a price here. Usually the price is small. A little begging. A little degradation. Some small bit of supplication for my amusement. It's nothing you won't happily give me."

"Master, please touch me," she whimpered. "Please."

He moved in closer and pressed his hand against the side of her cheek. She leaned into his touch.

"Like this?" he teased.

"N-no . . . please. I need . . ."

"I know exactly what you need. You need to be a good little slut for me, don't you?"

If anyone else had spoken to her that way she would have been horrified. She would have been horrified if Hades had done it a few hours ago, but she was so desperate for him to put his hands on her that he could say anything he wanted. He could order anything, and she would obey him. Not out of fear but out of the complete clawing need that ached from between her thighs.

"Please, Master."

"So you'll be a good little slut for me?"

"Yes . . . yes, I'll do anything." She squirmed on the leather, trying to pleasure herself but she knew it would never be as good as him touching her.

"You'll do anything I ask?"

"Yes."

"In front of anyone?"

"Yes."

"With anyone?"

"Yes," she panted. "Please."

He leaned in and took one nipple into his mouth and sucked, causing a thrill to shoot down her spine.

Then he untied her. Her legs ached as she unfolded and stretched them. Hades rubbed the soreness out of her arms and wrists and softly kissed the places where the ropes had chafed her. He moved the bench out of the way and climbed on top of the table with her, stripping his own clothing off as he went.

He was as beautiful without clothes as he was with them. He was all dark broad shoulders and finely chiseled muscle. Between his legs was the most perfect piece of male flesh she could have imagined, but he was so large it frightened her a little. She was sure he couldn't possibly fit without ripping her apart. Even so, she was more afraid of him not touching her, of leaving her in this needy unfulfilled state forever.

Hades pressed her back so that she lay on top of the pile of pillows and blankets looking up at him.

His eyes had taken on that terrifying glow again. "Hold onto either end of the table. If you move your hands, I'll stop."

Persephone gripped the edges of the leather table while Hades spread her legs wider, an evil smile lighting his face. She knew she was all his now. There was no part of her that could have resisted him.

Despite how long they'd been there, and despite how aroused he clearly was, he was in no hurry. He seemed to find as much pleasure in dragging out her torment as he found in the sex act itself. Otherwise he would already be inside her.

His dark hand closed around her pale throat. "Who do you belong to?"

Her breath hitched.

"Y-you, Master."

He loosened his grip and began to gently stroke her breasts and her belly. One hand lingered for what felt like forever on her hip.

"Please," she whimpered arching her hips up.

His hand moved with aching slowness between her legs. "Is this what you need, Sunshine?"

She bit her lip and nodded.

He stroked her gently for an endless span of time. Whenever she felt she was getting close to something, he would
pull back, slow down, stop altogether until she begged him
some more. He dragged it out, pushing each of her nerve
endings to the breaking point.

"Please. Harder."

But instead of touching her harder with his fingers, he
moved his head between her legs and started to lick over her
swollen bud. He held her firmly in place while he took his
time devouring her. She felt herself open further as his
fingers pushed inside.

"Come," he ordered.

She gripped the sides of the table, as if it were the only
thing that would anchor her, and then something that had
been clenched tightly inside her released, allowing waves of
pleasure to crest over her. Hades refused to let her go until
he'd forced her to accept the full overwhelming severity of
her orgasm.

Her grip on the table loosened while her breath struggled to go back to something like normal.

"How will you repay me for this pleasure," Hades asked,
the wicked edge back in his voice.

"What do you want?" Her heart still fluttered wildly in
her chest.

"Your innocence, of course," he said.

Persephone was pretty sure that was gone. But she knew
what he meant. He wanted to take her virginity now.

"I want you on your hands and knees. I want to take you
from behind."

Something clenched low in her gut as she remembered
watching the stranger fuck the woman that way and the
things Hades had said about it, how animal it was, how right

it was for her to submit to him so sweetly. And she knew he wanted that same surrender from her.

Persephone moved onto her hands and knees, opening her legs for him.

"Good girl," Hades whispered in her ear. "I'm sorry, but this will hurt."

She had known it would. Obviously.

Then he added, "But it's the kind of pain you'd beg me to give you again, so savor it. It only happens once."

He thrust into her, and it did hurt as promised—a sharp ripping pain that seemed for the smallest moment like the end of the world. She felt something break inside, but it didn't feel so much like an injury as an initiation. He remained still inside her for several seconds until the pain eased away, and then he began to move.

His thickness filled and stretched her to an impossible degree, but it felt right and complete.

She hadn't expected another orgasm. She wasn't sure she was even capable of it right now, but as he drove into her, Persephone felt another kind of pleasure and pressure building. This time it came from deeper inside her. It was so deep that she wasn't sure if she could handle it. It seemed too big for her, too scary to hold onto.

But then Hades leaned in closer to her. "Just ride it with me," he said.

He held her flush against him as he fucked her harder. This time when the wave built, she couldn't have resisted it if she tried. He let out a deep guttural sound as he came, and then she did with a sound nearly as primal as his own.

Hades pulled out of her and took her unresisting body into his arms. They lay like that together for a long time in total silence, her head resting against his chest as his heart beat steadily against her cheek.

Hades had all but discarded the original plan. Why should he make Persephone suffer for her father's sins? He could make Zeus suffer fine by keeping her down here, just by corrupting her innocence. And there were so many delicious avenues of corruption for someone who'd been kept as pure and untouched as his Persephone.

She thought her innocence was gone? Hardly. She was still so sweet and untainted by darkness, but he would fix that. She would become his perfect creature of the dark. He could taste it on her. Feel it. Smell it. Yes, corrupting her was much better. He could torment her, and he could make her love every second of it.

Things were awakening inside her already. Everything Zeus had spent thousands of years trying to stop, the innocence he'd painstakingly worked to preserve . . . it had all come apart in a matter of hours. All it had taken was for a dark god to touch her, and all the dirty temptations and desires came bubbling to the surface.

A woman's voice broke the silence of the room. "My Lord, what about this fabric?"

Hades looked up. He'd been so lost in his schemes he'd forgotten what they were doing. Persephone stood nude like a statue on a pedestal in the center of the downstairs parlor. The moonlight shone in through giant picture windows, illuminating her pale perfect skin.

She was so unbelievably beautiful. How could he deserve this creature? The fates must have seen the unfairness of the way the powers were split. She soothed every discontent. All he wanted was to be inside her forever.

"No. I want something more sheer." He wanted to show her off.

The woman nodded. "Yes, I've got something, I think."

He'd sent for a dressmaker to take Persephone's measurements and create something for her to wear to the party. She had already grown comfortable inside her own naked skin. She'd be fine here; already she was adapting so well.

The dressmaker stretched a glistening sheer silver fabric across Persephone's breasts. "How about this?"

Her dark pink nipples were clearly visible through the fabric. Not an inch of her would be hidden.

"Perfect. Can you have it ready in time?"

"Yes. It will be no problem, My Lord."

The dressmaker rolled the slinky glistening fabric back onto the bolt. Her fingertips brushed across Persephone's breast. Hades wasn't sure if it was intentional or not, but Persephone leaned almost unconsciously into the touch, then caught herself—and Hades watching with interest—and blushed.

The woman left them then.

When they were alone, Hades said, "You shouldn't be embarrassed. You may have all the carnal delights you want down here. I will withhold nothing from you and no one. In fact, I would enjoy watching you being enjoyed by others."

Her face went an even darker shade of pink, and she looked down, crossing her arms over her chest as if she could hide anything from his gaze.

"Would you like to play with some of my guests at the party?"

"I-I don't know," she said. But the flush moved into her breasts, and he could see her breathing deepen and the pulse jumping rapidly in her throat.

He moved closer and pressed his hand between her thighs. Warm, wet. So ready for anything. "Well, you just let me know. I would be happy to accommodate any desires you develop here. Just remember, Sunshine, there is no shame in the underworld. Only pleasure."

He was already completely lost. He couldn't bring himself to keep her in a cage or chop off parts or spend all his time terrifying or starving her. He thought he would want those things to appease his wrath and the suffering of nearly a thousand years. But he found all he wanted was to spend every moment teaching her body how to please him. And then rewarding her for her good efforts.

Hades watched with some amusement as Persephone's face contorted in pleasure, then confusion, and finally a little distress.

"W-what are you doing?" she asked, glancing around the room, clearly rattled.

"Me? Not a thing." It was true. He wasn't doing anything to her, but he had some idea what was happening. Still, it was so delicious to watch it unfold.

"I-it feels like . . ." She was becoming more and more flustered by the moment.

He smiled. "Yes?"

Persephone moved off the platform she'd been standing on and to a nearby sofa. Her breathing came heavy as she tried to cope with her new reality. She lay back against the arm of the furniture, her legs falling open. Such a lovely sight.

"It feels like . . . h-hands touching me." Her hips arched up to meet the invisible hand that must have been stroking her between her legs.

Hades chuckled. "So then I guess you *do* want to play with my party guests."

It appeared to take all her concentration to focus on the conversation. Every few moments she seemed to get lost in the sensations and give in to them. "Stop it," she panted. Then, remembering who she was speaking to, she added, "Please."

"I told you, I'm not doing it. I also told you the castle knows what you want. If you want the phantom hands to stop touching you, then stop thinking such unforgivably depraved things."

Her current predicament was within her power to stop. All she had to do was think something sweet and innocent, or just not think about fucking all his party guests as she obviously was. This was all within her mind, manifested and made real for her by the mind of the castle.

He certainly would have a talk with the castle later. After all, he didn't want her becoming too addicted to things which weren't real. He wanted her focus to be on the real sensations he and others could and would give her. But for now, for just this once, he would enjoy this show and the particular quirks of his home.

She gripped the back of the couch with one hand as her head fell back, and a moan escaped her lips. Her nipples were erect, and Hades could see the wetness gathering between her legs as she moved with the invisible hand.

"How many hands would you say are on you right now?" Hades asked. If he couldn't see inside her mind and he couldn't know with any great detail what she was feeling, he wanted data points. He wanted to know just how filthy her mind was.

She squeezed her eyes shut as if trying to concentrate against the sensations. "E-eight . . . n-no . . . ten."

"Are they male hands or female hands?"

"I . . .I don't know. Both I think."

"Tell me what they're doing."

Her blush went deeper. Talking about it seemed to be more difficult than lying back on his sofa and just taking it.

"Tell me, or I might have to punish you," Hades said. He might have to do that anyway. When he'd decided to corrupt her, he'd thought it would take more time, that she might be more reluctant. But in the end, it had taken such a small push, and her inner slut was already flourishing. He loved it. He never should have doubted the seer. Persephone had been made for him.

"They're all over me, rubbing and . . . and penetrating . . ."

It was all she could manage. Hades decided to be merciful and not demand further information. Besides, from the way she moved and squirmed, he could tell much of what was happening on his own. Both her little ass and cunt were being fingered while still another hand seemed to be moving feverishly over her clit.

"It can all stop if you think about something else. The castle is only giving you what you want after all. You could make it stop, or you could just go ahead and let it happen. I think you want to let it happen." He stood right over her, his arms crossed over his chest as she whimpered and mewled and bucked against the air.

She was too far gone now.

In another moment, he was proven right when a scream left her throat, and she rode the orgasm until she was wrung out.

After it was over, Persephone collected herself, scrambled to sit up on the sofa, and looked down at her lap.

"Well, did you have a good time? I'm sure it'll be even better when you do it with real people at the party."

Her head snapped up, her eyes meeting his briefly before going back to her lap. "M-Master, I can't . . ."

He laughed. "We will see. But you want to, don't you, Sunshine? You want to be my good little whore at the party. And nothing will please me more than to accommodate that insatiable appetite of yours."

He lifted her chin so her eyes met his. Then he surprised himself by leaning forward and pressing a soft kiss to her lips. She responded, her lips parting beneath his, a soft gasp drifting out of her. He sat beside her and pulled her into his arms. He couldn't be farther from his original plan with her, and he couldn't bring himself to care. All he wanted now was to teach and give her everything her heart and body desired.

Five

Persephone sat at the table in the dining room eating breakfast. Hades was away but had promised it would only be for a couple of hours. Her skin itched and felt too tight with him gone.

She'd been in the underworld now for a week, but it felt like so much longer.

Once she'd gotten settled into a routine, Hades had taken her on a tour. He'd started with the castle, showing her all three levels. The bottom level was the dungeon rooms, like the one she'd been kept in for a short while on her arrival. That part of the tour had been thankfully short.

The main level held the long entry hall, the ballroom, the kitchens, several parlors and casual living spaces, the dining room, and a library. Off the back of the library was a garden. Or it would be a garden if anything grew. Instead, it was a maze of tangled black branches, interspersed with white marble statues of grotesque beings—like what she imagined a demon might look like. And there were several benches to sit on.

After the castle, he'd shown her his kingdom, or at least the nearby places. The full domain of the underworld was as vast or maybe even more vast than the mortal world she'd known. And there were many different levels. Some places were about punishment and pain and suffering. Those places were far from the castle, and Hades had spared her having to see them.

Sometimes people got out of those places, but mostly they didn't. Everything else was a type of shadow life. It wasn't hard to see how someone could find enjoyment in this place. And Persephone was sure that for beings who weren't still alive like her, that the darkness must not be a problem. Maybe after death one no longer felt the craving for light.

There was no beautiful perfect place of light and happiness—no place like Heaven. Maybe there was a heaven, but if such a place existed, it wasn't in the underworld. But for most, this place wasn't hell, either. It was just an existence. People took their pleasures where they could find them—maybe in some ways not so different from life.

There were countless cities. Hades had only taken her to a few nearby ones. Some of them were all lit up like a carnival under the bright moon and stars, others seemed abandoned and haunted. There were areas with thick fog and tangled gnarled trees much like the forest they'd had to go through to reach the castle. And then there were places with rolling hills and pure clear starry sky for miles and miles. There were underground cavern cities as well.

Hades called that level the pleasure caves. Persephone didn't ask why. She could guess. When she was with Hades, she felt a twisted sort of attraction to the underworld. Although all the plant life and trees were dead, there was a desolate barren beauty to the way the tree branches entwined together as if clutching onto each other for safety.

There were some animals in the underworld beyond the horses from the castle and the giant three-headed monster dog—though Hades said most were just gone when they died. Animals didn't cling and beg for life like humans did. But sometimes they crossed over into the underworld. When they did, they mostly hid in the forests or the abandoned towns. So if there was a songbird or kitten out there, Persephone hadn't yet seen or heard about it.

Although a gloominess often settled over the underworld, there was good food, and pleasure, and fun to be had. And an eternity in which to have it.

The underworld felt like a black mirror of the world she'd known. Above, on the surface, she'd been sweet and innocent. Down here, she was something else entirely.

She wasn't sure which version of herself was real. Was it the sweet girl who didn't even think about sex, or was it this carnal beast she became with Hades? Either thing could be the truth. If it was true that Zeus had taken her desires away while he'd been hiding her—if any of that were even true— then perhaps Hades had been a strong enough catalyst to bring her back to herself.

Or maybe she truly had been innocent, and Hades was *doing something magic to her*. Maybe both things were true. Maybe both men had manipulated her desires for their own purposes. One to keep her pure. The other to corrupt her.

Hades was out, busy with last minute party preparations. The party was tonight. Of course, it was always night in the underworld—but the party was scheduled for tonight according to the time in her world. Her life in New York already felt like a distant memory, but still she missed it.

She tried to focus on finishing her breakfast—a buttery pastry, fruit, and coffee. But she couldn't. Every bite was harder to choke down than the last as she felt the lump forming in her throat and the tears begin to spill down her cheeks.

A female servant left her post in the corner and rushed to Persephone's side. "It's okay, Your Grace. He'll be back very soon. You should try to finish your breakfast."

"I'm not very hungry. I think I'll go up to my room and rest for a while."

"Of course, whatever you like."

"D-don't tell him. He can't know about this." Persephone was afraid for Hades to know just how much power he truly held over her. He couldn't know that his absence made her fall apart like this. He might use it against her.

The servant looked torn, but finally she said, "I am commanded to follow your instructions, so I will do as you wish. But if you will pardon my intrusion, you should talk to him about this. He has a right to know."

"Just don't say anything. It's a matter between us." She tried to sound as regal as possible, hoping her words might sound as if they could carry some threat.

The servant nodded quickly.

Persephone left the table and climbed the steps back to the room she shared with Hades and shut the door. Those stairs felt like climbing a mountain. She was so exhausted. The guard outside her door had raised an eyebrow at her struggle, but beyond that he hadn't said anything. Would she have to worry about him talking? What about the castle itself? The castle was a little too sentient in its own right for her comfort. Could it tell on her to Hades? Or would it follow her wishes and keep quiet?

But if the castle hadn't told him yet, surely it wouldn't now. After all, since the very first time Hades had touched her, she'd been trying to cope with the deep crushing sadness that swept over her whenever he stopped. When his hands were on her, everything felt right. She was indescribably happy. Everything in her head was songbirds and warmth. Safety and security. Peace. Sunshine.

For his part, despite the obedience he demanded of her, there were tender moments that made her believe something inside him had softened to her as well—that this overwhelming need wasn't one-sided, and that whatever was dead and broken inside him was becoming whole again. But at what cost? Each time he was away from her, it became harder to exist, to breathe down here.

He would find out eventually, and then what?

She stepped out onto the balcony. That stupid bright full moon. And darkness. No wind. No rain. No sunlight. Ever. God, she was drowning down here. Suffocating. She went to the edge and looked down. She should just throw herself over.

This place was so much less beautiful when he was gone. It was as if his very presence cast a sort of glamor over the place to make it tolerable. But whenever he was gone, all she could see was the wrongness of it.

She wasn't sure if she was truly immortal like Hades said, but even if she wasn't, wouldn't she come back here to this terrible dark place if she jumped? Maybe there was another, better place her soul could go? Heaven? Some way she could escape. No. It wasn't worth the risk. Somehow she knew she'd just end up back here. She'd always end up back here.

She took a deep breath and closed her eyes, trying to shake these taunting feelings. He would be back soon.

Everything would be okay. He would hold her and stroke her and fuck her, and everything would be right.

Persephone went back inside and ran a bath. That's what she needed. A nice, hot bath to make this feeling go away. But what if it never went away?

Stop being ridiculous. He's coming back.

Inside the tub, she let the warm water embrace her as she leaned back against the edge. She tried to think about the party and all the guests and the dirty things they would do together. She wished the castle would listen and distract her again with those disembodied hands.

It was funny how much it had disturbed her the one time it had happened. And now she wanted it to. But it never happened again after that first time, and a part of her thought it was some magic thing Hades had done himself, like so many other magic things he did. It was hard to know what was real with him. Everything felt like a grand illusion, a sleight of hand. The harder she tried to look and pin down anything real, the more wispy and elusive it became.

The water made a gentle gurgle as she raised her arm out and ran her fingertips over the silver collar at her throat. At least this was real. It was the one thing she could count on. When he'd first put the collar around her throat, all she could think about was how to get out of it.

And she didn't just mean the physical piece of metal. But out of this enslavement, this captivity.

It didn't take long, however, for the collar to feel like the only anchor she had in this strange, gnarled world of death. Knowing that she belonged to him began to be a real comfort. Watching the way his face lit up when she said *Master*, chased away any of the doubt she might have felt about the unconventional arrangement. He took care of what was his.

And if she'd thought it meant she was some lesser *thing* to him, she'd been dead wrong. If anything, being owned by Hades seemed to be the best outcome one could hope for in a place like this.

It began to feel like safety and security—the one thing she could count on. She felt so torn because she wanted to be free of this place. But the man? The god? Never. She *never* wanted to be free of Hades. In his arms was the most secure and happy she'd ever felt. And if it was magic, she prayed the spell never broke.

She finished her bath, put on one of the many black robes with the silver clasps that now filled her closet, and lay down for a nap, hoping to pass the time until he returned. But she couldn't fall asleep. She lay on the bed and stared out through the sheer fabric over the arched doorway of the balcony at the bright full moon that always taunted her in its crushing sameness.

It felt as though that glowing orb sucked all the strength and energy from her—at least when Hades wasn't there.

Persephone's eyes fluttered open at the sound of the door clicking. She glanced at the watch around her wrist. It was late afternoon already, edging into early evening. She'd slept after all. It had been a blank, dreamless sleep. She didn't feel rested. If anything, she thought she could sleep twelve or fifteen more hours and still not get enough rest. But then the door opened, and Hades stepped into the room.

He wore a black suit not unlike what he'd worn on the day he'd taken her from the city. He was loaded down with bags of things he'd picked up, no doubt, in a nearby city. His dark eyes took her in, and she felt immediately drawn to him.

He put the bags down just inside the room, and she got up and met him. When she reached him, she dropped to her knees. "Master." The word came out on a soft sigh, such relief to be so close to him.

Hades bent and pressed a kiss to the top of his head. "My sweet girl. Are you ready for the party? I have your dress."

If someone had asked her that a few hours ago, or even when she'd first woken up a moment ago, she would have begged to be left alone, the exhaustion so overwhelming that even the thought of doing something so taxing as getting ready for a party might drain her further.

But now, with Hades so close, she felt energized and happy. He was like the sun, warm and bright, and she seemed to draw life from his presence.

"Yes, I'm ready."

He took her hands in his and helped her to stand. When he touched her, it felt like electricity—as if he were charging her up like a battery. As soon as he let go of her hands, she put her arms around him and trailed kisses over his neck, his face, his lips. He stopped her, holding her in place for a longer, deeper kiss. She moaned and melted against his mouth, wanting to keep this one moment frozen forever.

"You didn't miss me, did you?" he teased. "I was only gone a few hours like I promised."

She wanted to tell him what happened to her in his absence. She just . . . couldn't. In the beginning, she'd thought he knew, even that he might be doing it to her on purpose to somehow addict her to him. But now she was sure he wasn't doing it. And if he was, he didn't do it on purpose. And he definitely didn't know about it.

Maybe he could be the world's greatest liar, but he wasn't a stone. He had feelings. She didn't believe he could pretend ignorance of her pain so well, especially when lately he seemed to want to cause her pleasure.

No, it was the underworld. The place was too dark and filled with death, too oppressive for her to live in it. This wasn't a place for the living, only for the dead—and somehow, Hades, who straddled both states. It was just . . . wrong for her to be down here.

Persephone was beginning to believe he felt something real for her—the same thing she felt for him. If it was all just magic, they seemed equally swept away by the spell. And wasn't chemistry a type of magic? Maybe this was the chemistry of gods.

Hades unlatched the clasps and pushed the robe off her shoulders and to the floor.

He took a black box out of one of the larger bags in the pile. It had a red satin bow on it. He laid the box on the bed and stepped back. "Well, go ahead," he said.

Persephone loosened the ribbon and opened the box. Nestled inside black tissue paper was the most amazing dress she'd ever seen. It looked like the long, simple gowns goddesses were pictured wearing in books on mythology. Except instead of white, it was that silver, slinky, glimmering, sheer fabric the dressmaker had held against her skin.

The material itself seemed to be made from a sort of magic. The way it glittered and glowed. The way it moved. It wasn't natural. It wasn't something that could exist in the world she'd come from.

Hades helped her into the dress and guided her to stand in front of the mirror. Her long blonde hair was the only shield she could have had to protect the smallest bit of privacy or modesty, but Hades pulled her hair back behind her shoulders.

She may as well have been naked because the dress didn't cover anything. It was merely glittering decoration to showcase her nudity. There was a high side slit on either side of the dress, which she was sure was meant for the easy access of whoever he shared her with. The thought made her heart leap into her throat. He'd assured her everything was okay down here, that one's wildest fantasies could be lived out without consequence or guilt or fear of judgment or reprisal.

Before him, she hadn't had any wild fantasies. Now it seemed that was all her mind could conjure. It was as though something inside her felt compelled to make up for lost time.

Hades leaned closer, his hands resting on her shoulders. "What do you think, Sunshine?"

"I-I look like a goddess."

He kissed the side of her throat. "Such vanity." Then his eyes met hers in the mirror, more serious now. "You look like a goddess because you *are* a goddess."

Did she believe that yet? It was still hard without access to the powers she was supposed to have. Part of her remained sure he must have made some mistake—taken the wrong girl. And what would happen when he discovered she was a fraud? What might he do to her if he found out she was just a human and not this goddess he'd searched the earth for centuries to find?

"Should I change back into the robe until the party?" She didn't want to mess the dress up. It was the most exquisite garment she'd ever laid eyes on—even if it didn't keep a single one of her secrets. Still, when she looked at herself in that dress in the mirror, she could see what Hades saw— beauty and grace . . . something desirable. And she felt unconcerned by how many others might see it as well at the party.

"No, the party starts in little more than an hour. That gives just enough time for someone to help you with your hair and makeup and for us to have dinner downstairs. You'll need to eat something to get through tonight."

She had no doubt about that.

"I'm taking the rest of the party stuff downstairs. I'll send someone up. Then when you're ready, we'll have dinner."

Persephone closed her hands into fists, fighting the urge to chase him and beg him not to leave her. He was in the castle. He was just going downstairs. When the door closed behind him, she looked back into the mirror. She couldn't live like this.

He had to let her go. She had to tell him the truth, and he had to let her go. But she didn't want to leave him. Even if he would let her, how could she just go back to her life and forget the things Hades had already awakened in her? She couldn't go back to who she'd been before. As much as she loved that life, it wasn't enough now. She didn't want to live alone with a bunch of plants. She wanted to warm Hades' bed. If only his bed wasn't located in such a horrible place.

"Your Grace?"

Persephone looked up to find one of the female servants had quietly entered the room.

"Let's finish getting you ready."

Persephone nodded and allowed herself to be led to a vanity table. She didn't know the names of any of the servants or guards. They were like shadows. They were there to make sure she remained comfortable and to give her whatever she requested, but they weren't friends or confidants. It seemed inappropriate to ask their names, and there were times when she had the weird feeling they didn't have names at all.

It was as though they weren't their own beings. They belonged to the castle. It was as if they were part of the mind of the castle. Persephone shook that strange thought away as the woman put makeup on her face, painted her nails, brushed and loosely curled her hair, and sprayed a light mist of perfume on her. It was clear Hades had made all his preferences known, and the servant merely carried them out.

Not that Persephone could argue with the results. There was a light glittery dusting of blush and eye shadow and a creamy pink gloss on her lips. She looked young and fresh and alive—so much more alive than she felt when Hades wasn't with her.

When she went downstairs, he was waiting in the dining room. He stood and smiled and pulled her chair out. It was so hard to believe this was the guy who had locked her in a cage and been so terrifying that first night. There were long spaces at a time, where she thought she could see something in him that was worth saving.

Persephone stood in the doorway, taking it all in.

The table was already set with food this time. The candles were all lit. The fire roared in the fireplace. That awful endless moonlight shone in through the enormous windows. She felt irrationally angry about that. She wanted to throw a stone at the window as if shattering the glass could make the moon go away. Why couldn't she have sunlight? She was sure everything would be better if she could have sunlight.

Hades held out his hands to her, and she rushed—perhaps too quickly—into his arms. He was so warm and safe. Nothing could hurt her as long as he was holding her. She was sure of it.

"You look enchanting."

And he would know about enchantment.

They sat and ate quietly. Hades always sat right next to her, ignoring the regal chair set for him at the far end of the table. That other chair felt like it was miles away, but the one he chose left him just inches from her. She could practically feel his energy this close.

The food was what one might find at a formal banquet—large roasted birds, savory stews, homemade bread, and vegetables. Fruit for dessert. But not pomegranates. He hadn't served her pomegranates again since the first night in the cage. She'd never had that type of fruit before the underworld, and though it had been sweet and delicious, she hoped never to have it again.

"Won't there be food at the party?"

He placed a hand on her arm as if he needed to be touching her as much as she needed to be touched. "There will be food, yes. But I thought you might prefer eating early. These parties get a bit intense, and I thought you might be too nervous or excited to eat."

"Oh." It was true, she was nervous and excited already. She felt both scared of the prospects of what might happen and thrilled by them.

"Who will be there?" Persephone asked.

"Friends. Beings in positions of power down here. Some of my generals. Their consorts. Only the most important of the underworld. You do still want to play with my guests, right? I have great party games."

Persephone felt a jolt of arousal hit between her legs.

"Yes, Master. It's not that. I'm just nervous." As wrong as part of her remained convinced it was, she *did* want to be open to all the hedonistic pleasures of his world. Partly to please him but partly to please herself. It was a new hunger, becoming just as important as the need for food, and one of the few things about the underworld she liked.

Hades caressed her arm with the tips of his fingers. Persephone leaned into the touch, her eyes drifting closed for a moment.

"Don't be nervous," he said. "They'll love you."

It wasn't long after dinner before the guests started arriving. Hades went ahead to greet everyone and settle them in the ballroom before sending for her.

When he had her brought to the ballroom, she was afraid she'd have to go in by herself, but he stood waiting at the entrance, his cold, black eyes warming when he saw her.

Persephone peered in from the hallway. The ballroom was almost too much to take in. She'd seen it on the tour, but at the time, the room had looked abandoned and dead— unwelcoming. She hadn't wanted to go exploring too deeply because the empty lonely place had depressed her. But now all the cobwebs were swept away. The black marble floor gleamed. For light, tall candelabras lined the walls, and glimmering silver chandeliers with lit candles came down from the ceiling. If this weren't the underworld, she might worry about the fire hazard, but she was sure Hades had things well under control.

There were alternating white and black marble statues coming out of the walls in high relief. Images of monsters and of the damned. A few highly sexual. The candles cast their faces in eerie glows and shadows. In the middle of the ballroom was an enormous white marble statue. Persephone hadn't noticed it during the tour.

It depicted a huge man-like beast sitting on a large throne. His presence was so lifelike and intimidating it seemed as if he would bust out of the marble to come join the party. His hands were clawed. He had huge bulging muscles. Sharp teeth showed from his smiling mouth. And there were horns. Persephone was sure if he were real, his eyes would have glowed.

A large cock jutted out from between his legs, and several nude nymph-like women surrounded him in chains. It was hard for Persephone to tear her eyes away from it. Hades had the most distressing and yet compelling taste in art.

On a stage at the far end of the room, an orchestra played instrumental music—lush, dark melodies. It was the kind of music that made you forget all the reasons you shouldn't listen to temptation, the kind of music that *was* temptation. Along one wall was a buffet table with all kinds of wonderful-smelling food as well as a fully stocked bar. She didn't think she'd want to eat anything for a while, even though she'd only managed to eat a small amount at dinner. She was too nervous to eat.

At least fifty people filled the ballroom, though Persephone wasn't sure they were all—strictly speaking—people. Most of them seemed otherworldly and a little frightening. She hadn't expected that.

She wasn't sure what she'd expected but not quite this. It was hard to put her finger on what made some of them seem *not human*. It was a feeling, an energy. Some of the guests had solid black eyes . . . not black like Hades had where that was just their color—but eyes that had no whites. Others had eyes that glowed red like embers from a fire. Some glowed a different color like green or gold, though the glow wasn't constant. It came and went in small quick flashes that one could easily miss if not paying attention, or if they didn't *want* to see it.

A few had . . . horns? She didn't want to think the word *demon*, and yet that word kept floating to the surface of her mind. Visually their inhuman quality was subtle—not an overblown show. You could overlook it or miss it if you were just looking with your eyes. But the energy that crackled off them was another matter entirely. It made Persephone feel anxious.

She didn't think they were *evil* necessarily. Just as the underworld wasn't really *hell* like what she'd heard stories about in the human world, these beings weren't really demons in the sense she might have heard of either. But though they didn't seem purely evil, there was something dark about them, something that . . . disregarded the rules of human engagement. She was sure they didn't have the same moral restraints or moral reasoning as she was used to. If Hades hadn't been standing beside her, she might have fled for fear of what some of them might do to her should they become bored with the music, food, and conversation.

"Ready?" he asked.

Persephone nodded. She wasn't sure it was true, but what were her options here? Make a scene and flee? Embarrass herself? Disappoint Hades? She felt sure he wouldn't let some nasty down here hurt her. In a short time, she'd come to depend on him, and so far he hadn't let her down. As much as she missed the world of light and living things, Hades had shown her kindness.

As they crossed the threshold, the room grew very still, the music fading. The murmuring and chattering came to a full stop as all eyes turned to them.

"Allow me to introduce the goddess of spring, Persephone, and now also queen of the underworld."

It felt like such a lie when he said it, but she didn't contradict him, and nobody at the party seemed skeptical of her pedigree.

There was a fair amount of oohing and aahing and polite clapping that caused a blush to creep up her neck. Soon enough, though, the moment ended. The music started back up, party chatter resumed, and Hades pulled her into the swarm of underworld beings to make more personal introductions.

The first cluster of people Hades brought her to had two women and three men. Both of the women had dark hair, pale skin, and red painted lips that matched their red eyes. They wore long black gowns which accentuated slim, willowy figures. Persephone thought their fingernails might be more claw than nail. One of the males closest to her had those disturbingly black eyes. The way he looked at Persephone, it was as if she could fall into that penetrating gaze and get lost—more the lost of insanity than the lost of romance.

He was very good-looking aside from that. But when he spoke, there was a slight hiss in his speech that you could only hear if you listened very closely. Persephone could have sworn a forked tongue slipped briefly from his mouth. And when he smiled, his teeth were too sharp.

"Persephone, this is one of my generals, Melos. He does punishment work for me in some of the lower realms."

She was sure this sanitized version of his job description meant he was head of torturing the bad souls.

"Charmed," he said as he took her hand and kissed the back of it. "We've heard of you for centuries. I can see now why Hades practically tore up the earth searching for you."

Despite everything, when Melos touched her, her trepidation fell away, and she let him pull her closer. His mouth brushed against her throat in a second, more intimate kiss. She shivered when his snake-like tongue slipped out and vibrated against her skin.

Hades chuckled. "Stop sniffing her."

"I can't help it. She smells . . . delicious. Will you let me taste her?"

The throbbing between her legs intensified. A few weeks ago, in the human world, sex had felt like a blank slate, something confusing and not really desired, at least not enough to go to the trouble of seeking it out. But in the underworld, something new grew inside her—a deep sexual hunger that could never be contained or satisfied. The way they looked at her . . . the way they spoke. All she wanted was to give in to it and fall under their spell.

"You are my honored guests. Everyone gets a taste," Hades said. Such a polite host.

Persephone felt she *should* object to *everyone* getting a taste of her, but the more the idea lingered on the air, the more exciting it sounded. She was certain the rules of the regular living world didn't apply down here. As long as Hades didn't become disgusted with her and throw her away, there were no real consequences to any pleasure to be had with anyone at the party.

The underworld felt like a long, fevered sex dream, barely even real.

For a moment, she considered the awful way she felt when Hades was absent and was gripped with a terror that perhaps he would decide she *was* dirty and wrong if she did these things. He might decide he didn't want her anymore. He had seemed thrilled that she'd somehow made it to him without having been with a man. Wouldn't the thrill be gone if she were with so many now? She couldn't understand his excitement by her purity only to turn around and corrupt it so completely.

But when she looked at him, his face seemed lit up like the sun, a positively carnal grin on his face, a warm glow in his eyes. He had no doubts about this, and suddenly neither did she.

"Persephone?" Hades said.

"I-I'm sorry, Master, what?" She was sure he'd said something to her and she'd missed it. She blushed when she realized she'd just called him Master in front of all his party guests, but Hades didn't seem troubled by this. He seemed pleased.

"Ah," Melos said, "when I saw that silver band around her throat, I thought it might be a collar, but I didn't want to be impertinent. However did you get the sweet goddess of spring to agree to a kink arrangement? That is . . . surprising."

"Well, you know, I *did* kidnap her," Hades said.

The general smirked. "Yes. There is that. But, she doesn't seem too put off by the arrangement. That's what I meant. As sweet as she is . . ." He reached out and caressed her cheek. " . . . she seems to long for it."

Before Persephone could decide if she should be troubled by this conversation, Hades' hand moved to the back of her neck. She leaned against him as he stroked the skin there making her feel warm and content. "You'd be surprised how hungry this one is. She may be sweet, but there is a kernel of darkness in her that is so raw and needy. She needs to be touched. I've never seen anything like it."

Melos took this as further invitation and reached out to stroke her breast through the glimmering sheer dress. She'd forgotten how on display she was. The fabric pressing and moving against her skin when she moved made her forget.

Persephone leaned into the general's touch, a small whimper leaving her throat. She'd thought Hades would take her around and introduce her to everyone, but all the guests had come to her instead, forming a wide circle around them.

She felt Hades move away from her as Melos began to explore her body. His hands slipped gently beneath the dress to stroke the tucked away folds of flesh between her legs—the flesh that was swelling with excitement each time he rubbed it. He withdrew his hand and sucked one of his fingers. She blushed, realizing the trail of wetness she'd left behind.

"She really is delicious," he remarked.

Persephone looked back at Hades to catch a satisfied smile on his face. He motioned to a few of the servants, and moments later, they rolled an absurdly large bed past guests and into the center of the ballroom, stopping next to the statue.

"The queen must be comfortable," Hades said. He turned to the general. "Well? Entertain us." He sat on a large regal chair that was brought up for him . . . waiting.

Melos guided Persephone to the bed. "Let's get this gorgeous gown out of our way, shall we?"

A trail of goosebumps sprouted up along her skin in the wake of Melos' hands as he slid the fabric over her body. He passed the dress to a nearby servant.

Hades had left his chair and was beside her all of a sudden. She hadn't even seen him move. He withdrew a thin strip of black fabric from a pocket of his jacket and blind-folded her with it. His lips brushed the shell of her ear. "Just feel, Sunshine. Everyone is here to bring you pleasure. This is your party."

He urged her to lie back on the bed. Moments later, more than one pair of hands began rubbing oil into her skin. At first her arms and legs, then her belly and breasts. And then something slick and slippery was being rubbed between her legs, then deep inside her. Her hips arched off the bed, pressing harder into the hands. It felt so much like the time the castle had given her such similar sensations that she couldn't resist the urge to pull back the blindfold to see if it was only an illusion.

But Melos and two other strange men were really touching her. The general was the one whose hand she bucked wildly against.

"Oh, she should be punished for that," he said, his eyes meeting hers briefly. "Little rule breaker."

At first she couldn't think what she'd done. Oh. The blindfold.

"Indeed," Hades said. "We have a deviant on our hands it seems."

Melos pulled the blindfold back down over her eyes.

"Do you want me to punish you, my dear?" he whispered. "I'm quite good at it."

He pressed a hand against her cheek. All at once, images flooded her mind of the general whipping a chained nude woman. The woman appeared torn between enjoying it and hating it. As these images continued, the general pushed a finger inside Persephone. She moved eagerly against him.

But he didn't just give her images, he gave her knowledge to go with it. He pushed it somehow into her mind. The scene he showed her had been a sexual game of sorts. And yet at the same time, it had been deadly serious. It was one of his captives in the lower realms—someone there for true and eternal punishment. She'd pleased him, and before long, his punishments had developed an edge of pleasure which she struggled in vain not to crave. Eventually, he'd released her from her sentence and from the lower realms.

The general removed his hand from Persephone's cheek and the images stopped, then he removed her blindfold. Now the only thing she could see was Melos looking down at her.

"What do you think? Want to try it with me?"

Persephone bit her lip and nodded. She shouldn't want him to play that game with her, but she did. She couldn't get the vision and feelings out of her mind of that woman so helpless and scared, still succumbing to pleasure in the pain he gave her. The temptation of being lost inside such a space overwhelmed her—like a weird sort of freedom in the middle of her captivity.

"Hades, you have toys?" Melos called over his shoulder.

"You know I do. What's a party without toys?"

More servants wheeled in a large, square, dark, wooden box. It had all sorts of strange markings and symbols etched into it as if it had been forged with the darkest of magic.

Melos opened the box and started rifling through it, tossing items out onto the bed. "Put her in the chastity belt. I don't want anyone touching her until I'm ready for her to come."

One of the males helped her into a sleek leather chastity belt and locked it. Persephone looked for Hades' reaction to all this, but his face gave nothing away. He sat silently in the large throne-like chair, nursing a short stocky glass of an amber liquid. His eyes were locked on hers. He was still fully dressed, but she could see the outline of his erection, the one clue betraying his excitement.

She'd thought they would use the bed, but the general made her stand, facing Hades, her legs wide, her arms spread open over her head. The moment he'd positioned her as he wanted her, she jumped as a sharp sound like a whip sliced the air next to her. But the sound wasn't a whip.

It was black vines shooting out of the floor and ceiling on the general's command, restraining her in the position he'd placed her in.

He leaned close, that snake-like tongue darting out against her throat to sniff the edges of her fear. "If you want to look at things so badly, look at your master. Don't take your eyes off his, or your punishment will only get worse. And he won't stop me. He likes it too much."

If Persephone had any doubt that Hades was entirely pleased by the events of the party so far, those doubts were erased in the smirk that inched up the side of his face. If anything, it seemed Hades and the general had played like this together in the past, and Melos' ordinary job was merely extending from the lower realms into the party.

Without the blindfold, she wasn't sure what would be harder to look at, the other guests watching her being whipped, or Hades. His calm, silent stare unmade her. She knew he'd be disappointed if she looked away. As if she could. His gaze held her so hypnotized that she didn't see Melos pick up the whip. She didn't hear him move behind her.

It wasn't until the leather strip landed against her back that she jerked in the vines that held her. She let out a surprised gasp at the sharp sting that burned across her skin. It was harder than her first and only punishment a week ago with Hades.

Hades' smirk turned into a full excited smile as he watched her realize what she'd just signed on for.

After the first strike, she heard the whip slice the air the moment before it landed, each time feeling as though it seared all the way through her.

As the general whipped her, she was sure the leather would flay her flesh off, but though she cried out, and the tears flowed down her face, and her body shook in her restraints with each lash, somehow she knew her skin remained intact. Hades wouldn't let him truly harm her.

She knew it in the way he held her gaze. The general may be whipping her, but it was Hades who touched her and was in absolute control of her. Their eyes remained locked together, connecting them beyond time and place so that everything disappeared but the dark gaze she was lost in. Not the lost of insanity . . . a scarier lost. Persephone thought as they shared this intimate moment, that something had shifted inside her.

She didn't just need him near. She didn't just crave his touch. She thought she might be starting to love him. She hated the underworld, but she loved its master. How could she love the person who had stolen her from the sunlight and buried her beneath the ground in endless night? The man who had put a collar around her throat and made her body open to him and all the pleasure and pain he offered.

Hades took a drink from his glass, his eyes never leaving her. The tears streamed down her face, and she wasn't sure if it was the pain of the whip or the realization that she would do absolutely anything Hades commanded. She didn't even want to disobey him. She couldn't decide if her pleasure was for her or for his amusement. She didn't know if she liked the pain Melos delivered or if she took it because she saw how aroused it made Hades.

"She takes punishment well. Like a pro," Melos said.

"She's more than I ever dared to hope for," Hades said, his eyes not straying from Persephone's.

Her throat went tight at that declaration. All she wanted was to please him. All she wanted was for him to never stop looking at her like this.

The general ran his hands gently over the places along her back and thighs where he'd whipped her. Heat rose off her flesh, but though it had hurt, she remained sure he hadn't broken skin. He laid the whip aside, and then his hand snaked around to the front, pressing between her legs.

She knew he had some sort of powers from the way he'd put images and knowledge in her mind with just a hand on her cheek, but it seemed he had other powers as well. His hand resting between her legs began to vibrate. But even with whatever magic he was using, the leather barrier of the chastity belt muted the feeling so that her arousal crept higher and higher the longer he held his hand against her. She couldn't reach her peak this way. Still, she closed her eyes, straining, seeking it.

Melos whispered in her ear. "What did I say about not taking your eyes off your master?"

Persephone's eyes shot open, going back to Hades, who looked entirely amused and entertained by this. Again, his gaze held her in thrall as she thrust her pussy against the general's hand.

"I can feel the warmth of her cunt through the leather. She's hungry."

"Good," Hades said. Then he turned his words to Persephone. "Tell me you're my good little whore."

"I-I'm your good little whore, Master."

"So much sweeter out of your lips than mine," Hades said.

The vibrating sensation stopped, and she was no longer sure if it had all been an illusion in her mind, or if it had somehow been real. He moved his hand to her mouth, his finger trailing over her lip before he pressed it inside her mouth. She accepted the mock penetration and sucked, her tongue stroking languidly over his finger.

"I bet she's a fabulous cocksucker," he said, pressing a second finger into her mouth as she moaned and whimpered around them, still watching her master for fear that Melos might punish her some more if she broke eye contact again.

She was about to come out of her skin with need. Hades never denied her pleasure like this. The throbbing between her legs had grown so intense she was sure that if she could focus she could come just with her thoughts.

"Bring her to me," Hades said.

The vines disappeared back into the ceiling and floor, and Persephone fell forward, her hands catching her fall against the cool marble.

"Crawl to him," Melos said.

By this point, she was a quivering ball of need. When she reached him, he'd already freed his cock from his pants.

"I want my guests to watch you suck me," Hades said.

"Please, Master . . . I need."

His smile was warm. "I know what you need, Sunshine."

He motioned to someone out of her line of sight. Hands seemed to come out of nowhere to unlock and remove the chastity belt. Cool air hit the wetness between her thighs, driving her even more mad with need

"Please me, and they'll please you," Hades said.

Persephone didn't hesitate. She gripped his cock with one hand as she licked his warm skin. He seemed to pulse with as much desire as she did. He just had better control of his emotions.

As she worked his cock, she had a heightened awareness of being watched. Fifty pairs of eyes on her, watching her pleasure her master with her mouth. She got so lost in the moment that at first she didn't realize hands were on her, stroking every inch of her, spreading her legs wider. Her body trembled as a long tongue pushed its way inside her. The tongue plunged in and out of her, occasionally coming out to softly lick her clit.

Then the tongue was gone and someone was working a cool thick dildo inside of her. She closed her eyes and returned her focus to Hades, her head bobbing up and down on his cock in time to the phallus fucking her.

When he came, he petted her hair and murmured his approval. She didn't hesitate to swallow every drop, needing more and more of him inside her. A few moments later, her own orgasm came, clawing its way up from somewhere deep inside her belly. She screamed out her pleasure as she floated on the sea of hands stroking her.

After a few moments, the hands receded, the toy that had been inside her was gone, and she knelt on the ground between Hades legs, her head resting on his thigh while he continued to stroke her hair. They stayed that way for a long time.

But then needy hands began to paw at her again, and her desire to be fondled and fucked returned. There was no amount of pleasure that was too much, no amount of degrading debauchery that she wouldn't gladly submit to— all for her master's entertainment and to feed her own grow-ing appetites.

She felt herself being pulled up off the floor and taken back to the bed.

Most of the guests had started engaging in their own sexual games among themselves, but their attention never seemed to stray far from Persephone, as if what happened with and to her helped fuel their own lusts.

Hours passed like this with hands and cocks and tongues all demanding entrance into her body. Persephone gave them everything they demanded over and over again.

She couldn't see Hades now. She felt him near, but he must be playing with someone else. Strangely, that idea didn't bother her. After all, she was playing with others. Lots of others.

One of the males lubed the large marble cock of the statue next to the bed while one of the females rubbed more slippery cool lube inside Persephone's pussy. She didn't resist the two strong males who lifted her up and carried her to the statue.

She straddled the marble creature as the males helped lower her onto the thick phallus. Despite how much she'd been penetrated, the statue's cock was frighteningly large. It had required a lot of lube and the insistence of strong hands pushing her down over it to successfully seat the thing inside her. Several guests chanted for her to fuck it, exciting her more. She gripped the beast's shoulders and raised and lowered herself onto the marble protrusion.

"Harder," someone shouted from the crowd.

One of the males who'd helped her mount the statue, gripped her hard around the waist and raised and lowered her faster and harder, his speed and strength far more than a mere mortal could have managed. All she could do was hold on as the pleasure built inside her.

"That's right," he growled. "Come for us."

Six

Hades sat on a leather couch at the far end of the ballroom drinking another glass of scotch. Persephone was a big hit. She was everything he'd imagined and more. The gathering had turned quickly from pleasantries and polite pretense to a debauched orgy in nearly the blink of an eye—as he'd known it would.

It hadn't taken long for every stitch of clothing to come off every creature down here and for bodies to start entwining and clawing toward their pleasure. Hades was probably the only one in the room currently wearing pants. He wanted to at least look like he had some control of himself. Clearly no one else did. Not that he minded.

If an underworld party at the castle didn't turn into a full decadent descent into pure naked hedonism, well, he'd completely failed.

One of the servants crossed the floor with purpose, his gaze trained on the ground in front of him. When he reached Hades, he made a small bow and held out a silver tray. "My Lord."

On the tray was a small, white piece of paper folded over once, with a red wax seal on it. Hades took the note from the tray. "Thank you, you may go." He knew without opening it that this would not require a response.

The servant scampered off into the crowd. Hades broke the seal. He knew who it was from. Since he'd brought Persephone to the underworld, he'd had spies out in force watching the upper world. He'd told Nick to keep him informed when anything changed.

Hades had known almost the moment Zeus knew Persephone had been taken. The poor humans. It had been several days of unrelenting wind and rain and hail. Hail so big it hadn't been safe for the little mortals to venture outside.

The note contained a short, scrawled message.

He knows about the party.

Hades smiled, refolded the paper, and slipped it into his pants pocket. If Zeus was able to come down here, Hades would be in a world of hurt. Luckily, he couldn't enter the underworld. Hades had hoped word of the party would spread and reach Zeus, but he hadn't expected word would reach him this soon.

Her father would know Persephone was to be the centerpiece of the event. He would know all the many ways Hades would desecrate her innocence and all the many beings down here who would have their turn with her.

If the weather systems in the upper world had been bad when Zeus learned of his daughter's kidnapping, Hades couldn't wait to see the disaster zone knowledge of the party would inspire. There might not be a world left.

Zeus should not have spent so much time and energy keeping her pure. Didn't he know by now that the more tightly you controlled your children, the more wild they went when they were finally free? No one illustrated this lesson better than Persephone.

But Hades didn't want to think of Zeus and revenge all night, not when there was a perfectly good orgy happening. Several naked women practically crawled all over him, their hands rubbing up and down his thighs—consorts of some of his generals. One of them licked and bit at one of his exposed nipples.

"Please, My Lord," she whimpered. "Let us please you."

"Hades!" It was Persephone. A panicked, distressed cry.

He jumped up, causing them to tumble to the ground. It only took a few quick strides to reach her.

"Stop!" he ordered.

The under beings who'd been having their way with Persephone moved away from her instantly.

"My Lord, Hades, I'm sorry," one of the males said, cowering pathetically. "She was fine just a moment ago. We would never disrespect . . ."

"I know." This was perhaps too much for her too soon. Hades helped Persephone off the bed and led her from the ballroom to a small parlor out of the way of the main party. The room was quiet and empty.

"Sit," he said.

She sat on a sofa in the middle of the room, crying and trembling. A servant came in with a robe and draped it around her.

"Your Grace," a second servant said, holding out a glass of water.

Persephone took the glass and drank it down quickly. "Thank you."

"Leave us," Hades said. "And shut the door behind you."

"Yes, My Lord," they said, quickly obeying his command.

Persephone chanced a look up. "I-I'm sorry, Master."

Well, he hadn't expected that. Did she think he wanted her hurt and terrified? Maybe his initial plans had leaned that way, but even the thought of truly harming her had been far from his mind for a very long time. Now the thought of anything ever harming her made him irrationally angry.

He sat beside her on the couch and began to run his fingers through her hair. "What do you have to be sorry for?"

"I embarrassed you."

"Nonsense. Of course you didn't. I would have never left you with them if I thought . . . Did someone hurt you? I'll rip his head off."

Hades was being completely literal. He'd rip the bastard's head off and put it on a pike in front of the castle as a warning. And since all beings here aside from him were dead already, the poor fool would be awake and feel it the whole time. From everything Hades had heard, pikes weren't particularly comfortable things to have jammed into one's skull.

"N-no," she said. "No one hurt me. I just . . . it was so much . . . I got scared."

"I thought you were having a good time."

"I was. But then I started thinking."

Hades chuckled. "Oh. Thinking is a terrible plan during an orgy. No thinking is allowed. Just debauchery. I was sure I'd been clear about that."

A weak laugh from her. Better than nothing.

He wiped the tears off her face. "Tell me, Sunshine, what did you start thinking that got you so upset?"

She shrugged. She looked so vulnerable all of a sudden, like something that really didn't belong in his world. That glistening golden hair, those guileless blue eyes. Soft, sweet, pink lips. His pants tightened at the memory of them wrapped around his cock.

He leaned in closer. "Tell me," he whispered.

"It was all just too much all of a sudden. It was so overwhelming. And then I started thinking . . . how dirty and wrong this made me. And then what if you didn't want me anymore afterward?"

"Why would I not want you? I told you I enjoy watching you enjoyed by others. When you gave yourself over so completely tonight I thought . . . that's my girl."

"Really?" She'd stopped crying at least, and the trembling was gone.

"And you aren't dirty and wrong. You're in my world now. Everything tonight is absolutely right."

Everyone in the upper world had such stupid ideas about sex. Everything was so shameful. Those idiots would rather be exposed to gory, bloody violence than a little bit of wanton pleasure. He wanted no part of it. And soon Persephone wouldn't either.

Fucking fools, all of them. And that twisted way of thinking had been shoved into Persephone's brain while she'd been up there pretending to be human. It was the kind of thinking Zeus had. If Hades ruled the upper world, things would be very different up there. A lot more pleasure and a lot less angst and guilt over nothing.

If it was the last thing he did, he'd train that shit out of her forever. Whatever Zeus thought about any of this, and however it might disturb him, Hades' priority had to be getting rid of this lingering shame. No goddess—least of all his—should ever feel shame in pleasure.

He stood and helped her off the sofa. "Come. Let's return to our guests."

"But . . ."

He raised a brow. "But what?"

"They'll think . . ."

"They won't think anything. This is not the human world. Those rules don't exist. The only thing down here is pleasure. Do you want to please me?"

"Y-yes, Master."

He leaned in, breathing in her scent. "And I know you want to come. I can smell it on you."

She blushed.

Hades brushed aside the fabric of the robe and put his hand between her legs. "Your body wants to be a good whore for me. All this sweet little cunt wants is to obey me. Is that what you want, too?"

She whimpered and moved against his hand.

"That's it. Let yourself go for me." He let her reach the very edge of her orgasm, where only the slightest nudge would push her over the cliff. But then he took his hand away.

"Master, please . . ."

"At the party. Come back with me and play. I will stay with you the whole time."

She nodded. "Okay."

"Good girl." Hades guided her back down the hall and to the ballroom. "Would you like something to eat?"

"M-maybe a small piece of cake?"

He nodded and led her to the buffet table and cut her a small slice of chocolate cake. "Water or something else?"

"Water is fine."

He filled a goblet and took her to a private table in a corner near the band. The food seemed to ground her some and strip away the buzzing edge of anxiety. The last thing he wanted to do was to hurt her, but he couldn't let her hide inside herself and the sort of nonsense Zeus had wanted her to believe.

Persephone would fuck whoever Hades told her to fuck, and she would be blissfully happy every second of it. She would not be hemmed in by the stupid mortal rules she'd been taught to believe applied to her. Nothing beyond Hades' will and considerable appetites applied to her, and it was best she learn it early in their relationship.

Persephone ate her dessert slowly, and he knew she was stalling. It was absurd. She'd been doing so well, and he knew she'd been enjoying herself. Maybe it was difficult given the life she'd led and the lies she'd believed about herself. Hades still wasn't sure she accepted who she was. Without her powers, he imagined denial would be easy.

When she'd finished, Hades assisted her out of the chair and led her back to the enormous bed in the middle of the hall. The guests who had been engrossed in their own trysts, quickly disentangled themselves and followed him and Persephone to the middle of the ballroom.

He pulled her close and whispered in her ear, "Remember, my rules are different. The sluttier you are, the happier I am. I want you to fuck everyone at this party, do you understand?"

"Yes, Master."

He removed the robe and handed it to one of the servants, then he ran his hands over her, as if memorizing her. Goosebumps popped out over her flesh. Her nipples were erect, her skin flushed and ready to be touched. He bent and trailed his tongue over her breast. She arched against him and moaned.

Hades felt between her legs to make sure she was aroused. He was shocked by just how wet she was. It was exactly as he'd thought. Her minor freak out had merely been the result of getting lost in thoughts that had no place in the underworld.

"My Lord, Hades."

One of the servants had managed to slip up on him undetected. Hades was going to have to put a bell on that one.

"Yes, what is it?" He didn't need to be distracted right now. He needed to keep a close eye on Persephone after the earlier incident.

"I have another message from Nick." The servant held out a silver tray, his hand shaking a bit.

Hades took the crisp white note and broke the wax seal.

Zeus has plunged the upper world into winter and swears he will not return it to balance until his daughter is released.

Hades felt the glow come to his eyes. Sometimes he felt certain if he were to remain angry like this, he would incinerate from the inside.

"I-is there a message? He said I should wait for a message."

Hades sighed. "Yes, tell him to return to the underworld immediately. He knows where to meet me."

The servant bowed. "Yes, My Lord."

Hades turned back to the party. The orgy was still in full swing, and Persephone was going strong. But it wouldn't take Nick long to get back, and he didn't want to leave Persephone alone with his guests. He'd promised her.

He caught the eye of the orchestra conductor and drew his finger across his throat. The conductor nodded, and the music stopped. The rest of the guests were stunned into silence by the abrupt absence of music—at least those not too lost to other more consuming activities.

"If I could have your attention," Hades said.

Everyone stopped doing what they were doing. A loud moan rose from the group closest to him.

"Persephone, you too."

A few nearby chuckles.

"I'm afraid I'm going to have to cut the party short. I have business to attend to."

Disappointed groans rose from the crowd. And then Persephone, naked and flushed and pulsing with desire, stepped out from the group that had been attending to her considerable and growing needs.

"But Master . . ."

That pout. That lip.

"I don't want to leave you alone," Hades said. But who was he kidding? She'd long given herself up to the party. Whatever nasty leftover human feelings she'd had about the whole thing had disappeared by something like her tenth orgasm. She seemed to hum now, a buzzing energy leaping off her in sparks.

For a moment, he almost thought he'd seen her eyes glow. But without her powers, that was impossible.

"Please, Master." A sad little mewl. She was in full wanton bloom. It would be a crime to stop her now.

Hades' gaze swept the room. "The party continues on one condition. She says stop, you stop. If anyone disobeys the queen's wishes while I'm gone, there will be unspeakable torments waiting for them."

Persephone wrapped her arms around his neck and placed warm, wet open-mouthed kisses along his throat while she rubbed herself lewdly against him. At least he'd accomplished one goal tonight. Her sense of shame and modesty had left the building.

"Thank you," she practically purred. She was only making it harder for him to pull himself away. But somehow he managed.

He quietly enlisted a few of the servants to act as spies to watch out for her. He didn't leave the party until he was confident she would be safe. By the time he reached the gardens, Nick was already out there, sitting on a white marble bench next to some nearly desiccated rose bushes and a statue depicting a mortal being tortured by one of the under beings.

Nick stood when Hades reached him and bowed. "My Lord."

"Skip the formality. Talk." He looked especially twitchy tonight, and Hades didn't like it.

Nick was one of the few beings who could spend extensive periods of time both in the underworld and on the surface, which made him an excellent spy. Most mortals these days would describe him as a demon if they even believed such creatures existed. His job was to tempt the weak-minded, and for that task, he was allowed in the upper world—call it a visitor's pass.

"It's bad," Nick said.

Hades rolled his eyes. "What do I care what petulant tantrums that overgrown baby throws up there? He wants to destroy his own domain . . . let him."

"You *should* care. The world will last a year at most in the current conditions. Then everything and everyone will die. It will throw the entire balance off. And we can't process that many souls that quickly down here."

Hades picked up the statue and flung it across the garden. It made a satisfying shattering sound as it crashed against the hardened ground a few yards away.

"You're going to have to make a deal with him," Nick said.

Hades growled. "No. No deals. Fuck him and his deals. You go to him. You tell him I don't care what he does, I will *never* release Persephone. She is *mine*."

"My Lord, you must listen to reason." But Nick was already backing away.

Hades paced, his boots crunching over the shattered statue. "No, you listen. You tell him I am calling his bluff. If he destroys and kills everything, Persephone has nowhere to go, and he knows it. I think he enjoys the world too much to destroy it over this."

"But . . . all the souls . . ."

"I'll destroy them if I have to. And you tell him I said that."

Nick's face blanched. Destroying souls—simply snuffing them out of existence—was dark work, even for Hades. He'd only done it once or twice in thousands of years. And on a much smaller scale. The act had done something to him, chipped away a piece of his ability to feel. He'd been like cold stone for months after, only slowly recovering back to himself. And that had felt like a close call—like his single chance not to fuck it up again. A warning.

If he were to destroy millions or billions of souls at once? He was sure he would become something unrecognizable, which nothing could bring him back from. If he did that, Persephone would look on him with revulsion and terror. And she'd be right to.

If he did that, she might not be safe with him.

But he couldn't let her go. Zeus had to believe Hades was fully willing to go through with this. Therefore, Nick had to believe it. Whether he was or not, it was his only card to play because the alternative was unthinkable.

He wasn't returning Persephone. So it came down to the two master bluffs . . . killing the world with winter or destroying every soul winter killed.

"Go!" Hades said, his arm held out firm and unwavering as he pointed off in the distance, toward the portal.

Nick turned to obey the order.

"And Nick?"

"Y-yes, My Lord?"

"You tell that bastard that if he forces my hand . . . if he ends the world and I have to destroy all those souls . . . you tell him . . . If he thinks Persephone lives at the mercy of a monster now, he has no idea what he'll be subjecting her to if he follows through with this. If any part of him cares for her, he'll rethink this strategy."

If possible, Nick turned even whiter. "Y-yes, My Lord." And then he was gone.

Hades sank onto the bench, his head falling into his hands. Nick believed it at least. That meant there was a chance Zeus might.

He knew his eyes glowed. He was so angry that his perfect, human-looking visage was starting to fade. His hands began to form claws as his skin took on a black glistening sheen like a snake. He couldn't go back to the party until he calmed down. He wouldn't let Persephone see him like this. She'd already seen glimpses of it with the eyes. He never wanted her to have to see what he could turn into if he let himself go.

Everyone, whether mortal or god, had a pressure point. There was a thing that if unleashed took on a life of its own.

For Persephone, it was a beautiful lust that only brought good things to the underworld. In the full blush of orgasm, she brought life to everything near her. For Hades, it was anger, bitterness, all the rage he'd bottled for thousands of years. If he let that go, everything would burn.

If he destroyed all those souls, he might shift to that *thing* and never come back. And what if he hurt her?

He sat in the garden for hours breathing slowly and deeply, trying to get a handle on his emotions.

"My Lord?"

He looked up to find one of the servants he'd enlisted as a party spy standing a few feet from him.

Hades jumped to his feet. All at once, his hands went back to normal, and he felt the heat leave his eyes. "Is something wrong?"

"No, My Lord. The goddess seems spent. I thought it might be time for you to come collect her."

"Of course."

The party had thinned out by the time he got back to the ballroom, most of the guests having gone. The few that remained were drinking gin and sitting at a table playing cards. The band had long stopped playing. Persephone lay on a sofa at the far corner of the room near the guests playing cards, sleeping, the robe covering her like a blanket.

"She's been out for about twenty minutes. Poor thing is worn out," Melos said, an evil gleam in his eyes.

Hades had no doubt he'd helped wear her out. "Thanks for taking care of her." He scooped her up and carried her up to their room.

She stirred briefly when he put her in the bed. "Master?"

"Shhhh. It's time to rest."

Persephone let out a small sigh in response, and her eyes drifted shut. Hades undressed and got into bed with her. He pulled her against him and just held her while his mind buzzed with worry about the future.

Seven

Months passed. Slowly Persephone came to accept her place in the underworld. She had thought the party introducing her was a special occasion, but Hades held many more parties—nearly every week. And every week she gave herself willingly to her master's party guests. Each week she became more at peace with all of their carnal demands. She became more open, more free.

Her body sang under their touch and Hades' amused gaze. He played with her as well at the parties, but often waited until later to have her to himself.

She still missed the sunlight and living things—plants and flowers and all the buzzing bugs and bees that it was so easy to take for granted. But she had made peace with the endless full moon and all the stars that never faded into dawn.

Hades stayed close to her most of the time. She'd convinced herself that everything would be fine. She'd made things too big in her mind. What the underworld did to her . . . it was all in her head. She'd acclimated.

Perhaps it was just a period of mourning what she could no longer have. But this was her life now, and things were fine.

Persephone managed to convince herself of all this until the morning she woke to an empty bed. The little sun gleamed on her watch. The time was ten thirty. She'd slept much later than normal.

She touched the empty place where Hades should be. The bed was cool. How long had he been gone? When would he be back? She felt the panic start to claw up her throat. She took a few deep, steadying breaths. She'd been fine before she knew he was gone. This had to all just be in her head.

Hadn't she been getting used to the underworld? *Only with Hades near.* She'd come to accept the underworld as it was. All dark gloominess. Fog and stars and night all the time. Dead things everywhere.

She was sure she knew now why Hades had so many orgies. It was the only way to feel down here. Chasing pleasure constantly, mindlessly. Seeking more and more filthy activities. Skin oiled and sliding against skin. Fingers and cocks and tongues exploring. The thrill and high of all these games helped one forget for long spans of time that this was it. This was eternity.

Stretched out before her was an endless night with no hope of a warm sun on her face again. No hope of rain or birds chirping or plants blooming like magic, their fragrances wafting out onto the breeze. She'd taken it all for granted.

At the flower shop, just outside, there had been a tree on the sidewalk where a robin had built a nest. The week before Hades had come for her, the baby birds had chirped incessantly in the background. She remembered wanting them to shut up, and now she would never hear them again. If she could go back, she'd appreciate it more.

There was a knock on the door, and she startled. "Who is it?" *Please be Hades.* Maybe he'd just gone to bring her breakfast in bed. He had sweet moments like that. Sometimes it was easy to forget she was essentially his prisoner. Queen or not, he'd kidnapped her from the surface and hadn't given her much choice in her accommodations.

But it was only one of the female servants. "I'm sorry to disturb you, Your Grace. My Lord Hades left many hours ago on business. He may be gone several days. He instructed me to bring you this token of his affection and his apologies for his absence."

Persephone's heart hammered in her chest as she tried not to think about *several days* and how she would get through it. Instead she turned her focus to the large, mysterious gift that had been rolled in on wheels by two other servants.

The gift was tall and domed on top with a black blanket draped over it. The servant pulled the blanket off to reveal a large silver cage with a raven inside.

"You can let the bird out. It will always come back to you. It's charged to watch over you," the servant said. "You should come down for breakfast soon."

"Thank you, I will," Persephone promised.

When the servants had left, she opened the cage. The raven flew out and did a few swooping laps around the room then came to rest on Persephone's shoulder. She petted the bird and put it back on its perch in the cage, leaving the door open.

It wasn't the same as a songbird, but it was a bird—something she could pretend was really alive, even if she felt sure it was just the soul made flesh again by the magic of the underworld.

The raven tilted his head and studied her for a long while as if trying to puzzle her out. Then it began grooming itself.

Persephone wasn't sure how long she watched the bird or how much time had passed, but she forgot about breakfast. She wasn't hungry. The raven wasn't a big enough distraction, and her mind kept going back to the utter horror that Hades would be gone for days.

Days.

The most she'd been apart from him had been a few hours, and she'd barely held it together then. She felt now as if she were moving through a thick sludge of molasses. The air felt heavy and too hard to breathe. The darkness seemed to swoop down and engulf her. She wanted to scream, but the sound refused to exit her mouth. She tried to cry, but the tears dried on her face.

Persephone wanted to climb out of her own skin. She paced the room, but though it felt like she was moving furiously fast in her mind, in reality she moved in that achingly slow way—like she was dying.

Yes, she felt like she was dying in this place. Dark voices started to whisper in her mind, offering her death, release, peace, escape. She wouldn't last days. It was too much time. What if she just shriveled up and blew away in his absence?

She'd done her best. She'd fought as hard as she could to exist and be here, but now the underworld crowded in on her senses, crushing her. Suddenly, the entire vastness of Hades' kingdom felt like a small black box from which there was no escape. If she screamed, no one would hear her or care. No one could help her. She was utterly alone. She felt as though she were trapped at the bottom of a dry well, shouting up into a void, and there was nobody at the top to hear her.

Persephone left the bird cawing after her in the cage and went to run a bath. She slipped the robe off and got into the warm water. All at once, there was a small silver razor resting precariously on the porcelain edge of the tub. Yes, the castle knew what she wanted. What she needed. Escape. This was her ticket out. It was the loophole. If she couldn't get past the dog . . .

It didn't hurt. Nothing could hurt like the suffocation of the underworld and Hades' absence. She smiled at pink water. Color. Finally, color in the underworld. She drifted in and out of consciousness, lulled by a peaceful, fuzzy feeling. She didn't know how much time passed or how much time it would take.

All of a sudden, she felt herself violently pulled from the water as it sloshed over the sides of the tub.

"Your Grace!"

She slipped and slid on the marble floor in the puddles of water that kept splashing over the edge. She banged her knee on the side of the tub. One of the servants steadied her and helped her back to the bedroom. Then several others were there with gauzy bandages and ointments.

They wrapped her wrists. The bleeding stopped.

Persephone wondered vacantly if she could have really died. If she was really immortal like Hades said then probably not, but if he was wrong and she was just a human . . . then maybe? Either way, why should the servants flit around her so panicked? If she were truly a goddess then surely this was nothing. There was no need to be alarmed. It couldn't hurt or kill her. And if she were a mere human, why should they care? Obviously, Hades got it wrong.

Nothing around her seemed real. It all felt like a fuzzy dream. She was so tired. So unbelievably tired. She just wanted to sleep and sleep.

"No. Your Grace. Drink." A servant pressed a glass of water to her lips.

"Leave me alone," Persephone said, pushing the glass away. She wanted to go back to the peaceful pink dream, the comforting embrace of death that must have been coming. She could feel it. It was coming for her.

But they wouldn't listen to anything she wanted. They pushed and prodded until she drank the water down, and then someone else was offering her a warm sticky bun.

"You need to eat something," she said.

It smelled so good, strong cinnamon and warm melty icing that, for the smallest moment, she didn't feel the oppressive weight of the darkness. For one moment, it felt almost like springtime and the sticky buns Lynette used to bring in from a corner bakery on bright spring mornings.

As she ate, she was vaguely aware of the activity going on around her, the urgent tones of the servants.

"He has to come back," one of them said.

"Send the raven," another said.

There was a flutter of wings as a note was attached to the bird's leg, and then it flew out the balcony doorway.

"H-Hades? He's coming back?" Persephone asked.

"Yes, Your Grace. The raven will be quick, and I'm sure he'll rush right back."

Persephone wasn't sure what to feel. Everything seemed dull and unreal.

"The water is pink," she said absently. "It doesn't match the bathroom. Something must be done." She sounded more and more like a lunatic even to her own ears. All she could think was that Hades would see that girly pink water and have some sort of fit.

"Someone is already cleaning up the bathroom. Everything will be fine. Just rest."

Persephone couldn't think about anything beyond that, not even to decide how she felt about him coming back. She'd just needed to make it stop. It was too much. And *days* was too long. She couldn't do days like this. She barely held on for hours. Hades had to stay, or she had to go. It was the only reasonable thing. Surely he would see that.

She lay back against the pillows and stared at the gauze wrapped around her wrists. She was like a mummy. A partial mummy. Why was there gauze on her wrists again? She couldn't remember now. Everything felt so fuzzy and unreal. All she could remember was Hades was coming home and she was so very, very tired.

Hades was in the Northern Sector only a few hours' distance from his castle. He hadn't wanted to meet with Nick again in a place where Persephone might walk in. She didn't know all the drama her father was causing on the surface trying to get her back, and she didn't need to know. It would only remind her that she was his prisoner.

Besides a discreet meeting place, the trip also gave him a chance for a diplomatic visit with one of his generals. He tried to make the rounds regularly, especially to those whose work kept them too busy to attend many of his parties. Stavros hadn't even gotten to meet Persephone yet. The Northern Sector was a busy place, containing most of the souls of the dead. Average people trying to carry on their average lives as if nothing had happened.

Hades sat at a long dining table with Stavros along with his lovely consort Estella. Stavros had allowed Hades use of her while he was there, and she was just as yielding and charming as the general had promised—though it had only made him miss Persephone. As pleasing as Estella was, nobody was his goddess. No one else was so sweet yet so wanton.

He hoped to make his visit short so he could get back to Persephone, but realistically, it would be a few days. He didn't want to be rude.

The door to the dining hall flew open, and Nick rushed in. He glanced quickly at Stavros and Estella, then back to Hades. "My Lord, if I could have a private word."

Stavros and Estella quickly excused themselves. When they'd gone, Hades stepped outside on the back terrace. Nick followed.

Walls had ears in the underworld, and if what Nick had to say was truly private, Hades didn't want to risk anyone else hearing.

"My Lord . . ." Nick started.

Hades put a finger to his lips. "Shhhh. Not yet. Follow me."

Nick quietly shadowed him until they got off the property and into the woods at the mouth of a nearby forest of dead, black trees. Here there were only a few mournful owls to disturb them.

"Okay. This is good. What have you got for me?"

Nick had been keeping an eye on the winter situation, trying to convince Zeus to end it and bring the world back to balance.

"It's started."

Hades rolled his eyes. Nick could be so cryptic. He was sure he did it to drive Hades crazy. "What's started?" But deep down he thought he knew.

"The deaths. I haven't just been on the surface; I've been checking at the gates as well. We're processing too many souls too fast. Zeus hasn't backed down. Winter on the surface has grown more violent than ever. And now the consequences are starting."

Hades growled. "Does he not care at all about his daughter? I told him what would happen if he persisted in this."

Hades wasn't sure if Zeus hadn't believed him or if he didn't care. At the time, even Hades himself had thought he was only bluffing. But now he was becoming more and more sure that he hadn't been.

"You must return her to her father," Nick said. "He's not going to stop. He won't let you have her."

Hades laughed. "*Let* me have her? So all of this having her I've been doing for the past few months was all in my imagination? It seems like she's been mine for a while now. Besides, she ate the pomegranate seeds. She's tied to this place. Even Zeus can't undo that."

If Hades were honest with himself, he knew he still had some power to free her, at least temporarily, but those seeds made her his by right. Zeus wasn't winning again.

"Yes. I-I told him about the seeds. He still demands you send her back. There's no other choice. You have to send her back, and soon. We can't take this influx of souls. And it will only grow."

He'd been so wrapped up in Persephone lately that he hadn't noticed the increase. It shouldn't have been something left for Nick to discover. Hades hated being out of the loop in his own kingdom.

"There is another choice."

Nick's eyes widened. "My Lord . . . begging your eternal pardon but . . . you can't."

"Can't? You dare to tell the lord of the dead what he can and cannot do? You forget your place, boy. Return to Zeus. Tell him to end winter immediately, or I will start destroying souls. If he cares for his daughter's safety with me, he won't push me that far."

Nick looked as though he wanted to argue some more, but he was smarter than that. In the end, he only bowed and said "Yes, My Lord." Then he left to carry out the order.

Hades was about to return to Stavros' home when a cawing sound bounced and echoed through the trees. He looked up to see Persephone's raven swoop down and land on his arm. There was a small rolled-up piece of parchment attached to the bird's leg. Something inside him went cold, and a sick clammy dread grabbed hold of his heart. His hand shook as he unrolled the paper.

Come home. Persephone is unwell. Hurry.

He sent the raven back and mounted his horse. He didn't bother to give his apologies to Stavros and Estella for cutting their visit short. He would send a messenger back to them after he reached Persephone.

Hades drove the horse faster and faster through woods, over rolling hills and meadows, through cities and towns until, hours later, he reached the castle. The entire trip his mind had been abuzz with worry. What did they mean she was unwell? How could she be unwell? She was immortal. Gods didn't get sick.

He left the horse with a groom and took the front steps two at a time. He flung his coat at a flustered servant in the entryway. "Where is she?"

"Upstairs, My Lord."

Hades bounded up the grand staircase and then the second smaller staircase to his private floor and raced down the hallway to the room he shared with Persephone.

When he opened the door, he found her sleeping.

"What's wrong with her? What happened?" he demanded. One of the female servants rose from a chair where she must have been watching over her.

"We found her in the bathtub. The water was full of blood. She cut herself."

"Accidentally?"

"No."

He rushed to the bed, and as he got closer, he could see the white bandages wrapped around her wrists.

"She's okay. We just thought you should come home."

"Why would she try to hurt herself?" What did she think she would accomplish? Where was she going to go? Even if she could die, she'd still be in the underworld. It didn't make any sense. An irrational anger gripped him. Did she want to be free of him that much? He'd thought she was coming around. She'd seemed happy to him. Must he fight both her and her father?

The seer had promised she was his.

"Persephone!" He gripped her by the shoulders and shook her, but she didn't stir.

"My Lord, perhaps you should let her rest."

He rounded on the servant. "Get out. I'll handle this."

"Y-yes, My Lord." The servant and several others excused themselves from the bedroom.

Hades sat beside her on the bed and brushed the golden hair off her face.

"Sunshine, wake up."

He waited, but still she slept on. He shook her again, and her eyes fluttered open.

"Master?"

"What happened?" he demanded.

She seemed disoriented, as though the question were too confusing.

"What?"

He gripped her wrist, perhaps harder than he should have. "This? What is this? Why would you try to harm yourself? What were you trying to do? Were you trying to leave me?"

Her expression flitted quickly from her initial relief to fear.

"I-I don't know."

"What do you mean you don't know? Tell me why you did this!" He could feel his hands trying to transform into claws and the glow burning behind his eyes. He felt his teeth growing longer like a monster. It took every ounce of willpower to calm himself down and push the thing back down.

Then she started to cry.

Hades pulled her into his arms and held her and stroked her hair until she calmed, but the questions still gnawed at him. If she thought she could show him her pathetic tears and this would be over, she was sadly mistaken.

"Why?" he said quietly.

"I wanted to tell you the truth, but I was afraid you might use it to hurt me."

The more she talked, the less sense she made, but he forced himself to be quiet and wait for her to tell him more.

She took a deep breath. "When you leave me, even for just a few hours, I feel like I'm going to die. I-I can't explain it, but this place . . . Master, I'm not supposed to be down here. This place is only for dead things."

"I'm not a dead thing," he said, practically growling. Is that how she saw him?

"N-no. I didn't mean you. But you're a god."

"And you're a goddess."

She shook her head. "I don't have powers. I can't with-stand this place. When you're with me . . . when you're touching me, everything is fine, but when you're away . . . This place is killing me; you have to let me go."

Zeus had gotten to her somehow. Had he turned one of the under beings against Hades? Zeus must be feeding her the lines to say to manipulate Him. He had to be. It was all too convenient. Everyone and everything working against him.

"Never," Hades said. "You belong to me."

She started to cry again, great gushing sobs that she seemed to have little power over. It went on for several minutes until at last she gained control of herself.

"Then come to the surface with me," she begged. "Please. I don't want to leave you. The thought of leaving you tears me apart, I just . . . I can't be in this place. Surely you must understand that. I have to have the sunlight and the flowers and plants and all the things that belong to the living. I can't live here surrounded by death. Please. It's destroying me."

Hades searched her eyes for deceit, but he couldn't find any. She seemed to truly want to stay with him. Maybe Zeus hadn't gotten to her after all. But if these things were really happening just as she said, that was even worse.

"Persephone, listen to me, I can't go up there."

"But you were up there when you took me. And you said you searched for me for centuries, so you must have been up there a lot. Just leave someone else in charge and come away with me."

Hades shook his head. "No. It doesn't work that way. I had under beings searching for you. When there was a strong enough lead, I went to the surface to check it out myself. But I can only be up there a few hours at a time, then I have to return. It takes months before I'm able to surface again."

"Then you have to let me go."

Zeus, Nick, Persephone, they all sang the same refrain. *Let her go.*

It only made Hades cling more stubbornly. *Never.*

"No, I have to punish you."

She pulled out of his arms and scrambled back as far as the space of the bed would let her go. "W-what?"

"You heard me. You lied to me. You kept this suffering from me, and then you tried to harm yourself. Do you have any idea how furious I am with you right now?"

Her eyes widened in the first real fear he'd seen from her in a long time. Seeing her that afraid sickened him. But there was also something monstrous inside him that liked it. It would be so easy if he just let that thing out. He wouldn't have to care about anything anymore but sating his own lusts.

"You want to bleed, Sunshine? I can make that happen. If you're so fascinated with the sight of your own blood, believe me . . . I can accommodate you."

"N-no. I . . . I just felt so lost, and this place got into my head. It whispered things. I . . . I just wanted to make it all stop."

Hades took one of her wrists, and she jerked it back.

"Persephone, do not test me right now."

Slowly she held her arm back out to him. He unwrapped the gauze. The bleeding had stopped, but she was still far from healed. He had to get her powers back. If she had them, everything would be fine.

He re-wrapped her wrist and got up off the bed. "Come with me."

Tears slid down her cheeks. "Please, Master, I'm sorry."

He wasn't sure if he believed her. Whatever the underworld was doing to her, it had clearly driven her mad. He couldn't leave her again. If he went on business, he had to bring her along.

"I'm not going to make you bleed," he said quietly. "But I am going to punish you."

She scooted to the edge of the bed and pulled back the covers. She was still naked from the bath.

He led her from the room and down the hallway to the playroom. She didn't seem to even notice her nudity when she passed the guards anymore.

Inside the playroom, Hades raised an arm to the closet. It opened and a couple of large cushions floated out and settled in the middle of the floor.

"Sit. We're going to talk first."

If possible, she seemed to want to avoid talking more than whatever punishment was coming her way.

Hades sat on the other cushion across from her. "Tell me more about what happens when I'm not around."

Persephone was quiet for a long time, but finally, she started to describe all the various ways the underworld made her feel. Some of it was physical. A good bit of it was mental. But she was right, as things stood now, she was completely incompatible with the underworld. If he were better, he would release her.

Maybe it was right that he'd drawn the lot of the underworld. Maybe it was fitting.

"You'd be happier without me if I sent you back to the surface and left you alone," he said.

"I don't want to leave you. I just can't be here. I'm sorry I kept things from you. I was afraid."

Suddenly, Hades didn't have the heart to punish her. He only wanted to comfort and reassure her, but even that was too much. His mind was too busy, whirring with everything that was going wrong.

The honorable side of him knew he had to let her go. This place was destroying her. And yet . . . she'd eaten the seeds. Even he couldn't fully undo that mystical link. Would he if he could?

"I have to get out of here. I need some air." He couldn't sit here with her looking at him like that. He knew how much she needed him, but he just . . . he had to get outside and breathe and think.

"You can't leave me! You know what will happen."

"I won't be gone long. I promise. I need to think."

He ignored her panic and plaintive cries and bolted from the room. He didn't stop running until he was outside in the open air. He went to the stables and took one of the horses, and he rode.

He had to clear his head. It was all falling apart. Everything. Zeus was fucking with him. Couldn't just let him have this one good thing. Persephone couldn't be down here. And all the while, the seer's words seemed to haunt and mock him.

She is destined to be yours.

A pack of lies. How could she be destined to be his when everything was coming apart? If it were truly destiny, wouldn't everything fall into place? Wouldn't it be easier? He was going to find that seer, and he was going to fucking torture her.

He didn't know where he was leading the horse until he got there: one of the gates where souls were being processed. He should have stayed on top of this. He'd let everything crumble around him, and now the mess was almost too big to clean up. Fucking Zeus.

Nick was right. It was a swarm of them. Far more than usual and far too many. The underworld was in a slow and constant state of expansion, but there was a balance. An order. Zeus's eternal petulant winter broke that balance. He thought acting out would bring Persephone back? Zeus was a fool.

And if the overflow was bad now, it would get worse. This was just the beginning. Only the truly weak had fallen so far. But soon enough the strong would succumb, too. No one could withstand a winter without end. No one mortal, anyway.

"My Lord, Hades," Oris said. He was a low level grunt who had the boring and tedious work of processing new souls. "I haven't seen this many souls come through since the black death. It's crazy! What's going on up there?"

At least the whole underworld wasn't buzzing with the news yet. That was the last thing Hades needed.

"Oris, listen, I need you to do something for me." He wouldn't do it out in the open. Of course he wanted Zeus to know, and the smug self-righteous bastard would find out. But there was no sense causing unnecessary whispering in the underworld. No one needed to know Hades had lost it.

"Anything, My Lord."

"Randomly pick one hundred souls and send them to me. I'll expect them at the castle within the hour."

"Of course, My Lord."

One hundred wasn't nearly enough, but Hades was sure it was enough to make winter stop and fast. He wouldn't allow himself to think about what he would become, the danger he put Persephone in. Deep down he knew if he did this, he would no longer care how much she suffered. He could keep her without remorse. He could make Zeus back down, and he could keep her.

Eight

Persephone sat in a corner of the playroom, her knees drawn up to her chest, the tears streaming down her face. How could he just run off and leave her like that? This was exactly what she'd feared—that he would know the truth and still leave her to suffer.

She tried to take deep calming breaths as if she could fight and push past the suffocating oppression that crowded in on all her senses. If she could only find a way to survive when he was away. There had to be some coping mechanism . . . something. Maybe magic? Couldn't magic help her? This place seemed full of it.

She looked up suddenly. The energy in the castle had changed. Hades was back. She didn't know how she knew, she just knew. Like he'd promised, he hadn't been gone long. She got off the floor feeling stupid and melodramatic and wiped the tears off her face. She went to the bedroom and dressed in one of the long black robes from the closet. Then she raced down the stairs to meet him.

She'd expected to run into him. Surely he was on his way back to her. But their paths didn't cross. The hallway was clear. It was clear down on the main level as well.

She stopped in front of one of the guards lining the wall of the massive entry hall.

"Where is Hades?" She wasn't crazy. She felt him. She knew he was here. She knew it the same way she knew day would never fucking come here—that the sun would never rise for her again.

"Your Grace, he's ordered no one disturb him, including you."

Persephone was quite certain that was not the question she'd asked. How could Hades shut her out? She'd been kidding herself all this time. Whatever he felt for her . . . it was possession and control. It must be. It wasn't love. It wasn't like what she felt for him. She wasn't sure which was worse, to be stuck in the underworld with a man—no, a god —who couldn't love her, or to be without him and forced to face the endless night alone.

She paced back and forth in front of the staircase. He was somewhere in the castle. She could go find him herself. And yet . . . she was afraid to actively defy him and disobey his orders. He could simply leave her to her own private hell if he got irritated enough. He didn't have to break out the whips and chains now that he knew his absence was the greatest pain of all.

The castle's front entrance opened with a loud creak, and in drifted a crowd of people. A party? He was throwing a party at a time like this? But no, it wasn't a party. These weren't under beings. These weren't his generals and other high ranking officials and their consorts. These were . . . these were regular people. Souls who had passed on.

It had been so long since Persephone had seen regular people that she hadn't realized how much she'd missed the normality. Gods, demons, various under beings were not the same, even if they were people-shaped.

The souls entering the castle appeared lost and confused and afraid as they wandered down the entry hall. Was she supposed to greet them? Say something to them? But before she could decide what to do, one of the servants went to intercept them.

"This way," he said, smiling widely, "Lord Hades is eager to greet you."

The long line of people followed the servant down one of the main hallways to the ballroom. *Was* it a party? That didn't feel right. Something was wrong about this. She'd never known Hades to entertain human souls at the castle.

When the line had passed, Persephone started to follow, but the guard she'd spoken with stopped her.

"Your Grace, I have my orders."

"And what are you to do with me if I don't listen? Has he given you permission to hurt me or lock me up somewhere?"

The guard looked away. "No, Your Grace, but you really shouldn't . . ."

She stood straight and attempted to look as regal and intimidating as possible even though the guard was a full foot taller than her. "It is not up to you to tell me what I should or should not do. I am your queen. You forget yourself."

He offered a small bow. "My apologies, Your Grace."

She hadn't expected it would be that easy. No one else tried to stop her. When she burst through the doors of the ballroom a few minutes later, she wished they had.

It took a moment for Persephone to fully realize what she was seeing. The crowd of souls had been herded into the ballroom, and all of them seemed frozen. Some kind of magic held them, preventing them from trying to escape, because without it, she was sure they would try to escape. The tension in the room was so palpable, Persephone could barely breathe. It was too much like the feeling when Hades left her.

Hades stood in front of one of them, his hand outstretched, pressed against a man's chest. His hand glowed bright orange, and then the man screamed and . . . incinerated. There was a brief burst of flame on him, but it quickly died, and a neat pile of ashes were left on the ground in the man's place.

Persephone gasped, drawing all the attention in the room to her. "What? Why? How could you . . .?" Maybe they were bad souls. Like serial killers or rapists. But nobody inside the ballroom seemed evil. And weren't the bad souls punished? Wasn't that Melos' job?

"Bring me another one," he said. His voice had gone all dark and terrifying. Inhuman, almost like an animal. Before he'd at least made the effort of sounding like a person, but now . . . he'd given up all pretense.

One of the servants dragged another soul to him, this one a woman.

Hades turned to Persephone. He looked haunted, horrified by what he was doing. So why was he doing it? Why couldn't he just stop?

"Y-you don't have to do this," She said, even though she had no idea why he was doing it.

"Oh, but I do. And as much as it hurts me to see it right now, in a little while I'm not going to care about that look of revulsion on your face." He turned to one of the guards standing silently against the wall. "Get her out of here. Put her in the cage. I'll deal with her when I'm done."

She tried to run, but of course she didn't get far. His guards were so tall, with long, powerfully muscled legs. They could easily outrun her. It only took one of them to scoop her up and carry her down to the dungeon. He put her in the cage she'd been in the first night and locked the door.

"Please! Please don't leave me down here!" All regal pretense was gone now.

"I'm sorry, Your Grace. Truly I am. But I cannot defy him." Then the guard turned and left her.

No one else had been down here since her last imprisonment. The pomegranate she'd eaten that first night still lay in the middle of the cage where she'd dropped it, now dried and almost beyond recognition.

She tried without success to figure out why Hades was doing this. It couldn't be because she'd hurt herself. Or . . . was this her punishment? He had to know she wouldn't put other souls in danger. It wouldn't matter how much the underworld got under her skin, if she knew souls would be incinerated . . . she would never . . .

Could that be why? Oh God, could this somehow be her fault? Persephone moved to the back of the cage and sank to the floor, her back pressed against the bars in a futile attempt to steady herself. No, of course this wasn't her fault. Nobody was making him do this. But why? She'd come to learn he wasn't a monster. Hades wasn't evil. He had his darkness, but his darkness consisted of orgies and temptation, not mass murder.

She told herself she would never forgive him. She'd shun his affections. But he still held the only key to not feeling like she was dying in this place. How could she push him away when his presence and touch were the only things keeping her going? Though that might stop being true. She couldn't imagine still wanting to be near him now.

He couldn't come back from this.

She hadn't been able to stop crying since she was put in the cage, so she didn't hear the female servant come down.

"Your Grace?"

"Stop calling me that. I'm his prisoner. That's all I am and all I will ever be." It was such a joke to pretend she had any power here.

"That's not true," she said. "I-I brought you something to eat." She opened the cage a bit and pushed a tray inside with a sandwich and some water. "I thought maybe a little something might help. Nothing too heavy. I know you might not have much appetite right now."

That was an understatement.

Persephone thought she could probably overpower the servant and escape. But to where? There was no place to go that Hades wouldn't eventually find her, and she didn't want to think about what would happen then. She also didn't want him to hurt the servant girl.

The servant locked the cage again and started to go back upstairs.

"Why is he doing this?"

The girl turned back but stared at the ground as if she found the interlocking stones wildly interesting. "Please, Your Grace, I'm not supposed to tell."

"Tell me. It will be our secret."

She hesitated another minute but then she came back to the cage and sat on the ground near Persephone as if she were afraid to speak the words too loudly. As if Hades might hear her all the way down here and come incinerate her as well.

"I don't know all the details, but I've heard things. Zeus is trying to free you from the underworld. It's been winter on the surface of the whole earth for months now. And people are starting to die. He wants to flood the underworld with too many souls to force Hades to release you. So My Lord Hades is destroying souls to keep you."

It was the last explanation she'd expected. "So he doesn't care if I love him or hate him as long as I'm trapped down here with him?"

The servant shrugged. "I don't know what he's thinking. H-he's lost his mind. He hasn't been like this in a long time, and n-never this bad." The girl touched Persephone's hand through the bars. "Your Grace, he will . . . change. I don't know if he can come back to us. He may be lost forever. Whatever happens now, you must be brave."

"What do you mean? What's going to happen?" She hated how shrill and terrified she was starting to sound, but the servant's fear was getting to her.

"I-I have to go. He'll come down soon and . . . please don't tell him I was down here."

"I won't." It wasn't like Persephone could tell him much anyway. The only thing she could say was that a female servant had been down there to see her. The servants and guards in the castle were hard to tell apart sometimes. And she still didn't know anyone's name.

An hour or so passed. Persephone ate the food and drank the water that had been brought for her. It didn't help anything.

Finally, she heard heavy footfalls getting nearer and nearer. She knew it was him, but nothing could have prepared her for what came down those stairs.

It wasn't Hades.

It was a monster or a demon, maybe one from the lower realms—the places Hades shielded her from. He was enormous, and even with the high ceiling in the dungeon, he had to bend down to not bump his head. His skin was black and reptilian. His eyes glowed red. He had long sharp claws that were probably better described as talons. And there were horns.

She felt the pieces coming together as the realization hit her. It was the statue from the party. Had it come to life?

Persephone couldn't stop the scream that left her throat as the beast got closer.

"What's the matter, Sunshine? My true form too much for you? You seemed to like it just fine when you were fucking a marble copy of it at the party."

No.

"H-Hades?"

When he smiled, he revealed those too-sharp teeth—teeth that could easily rip fragile flesh like hers. "What did we say about that? You call me Master."

His voice wasn't his own. He sounded more monster than man when he spoke.

"H-how many souls did you destroy?"

"A nice even one hundred. And I will destroy more if I have to."

She crossed her arms over her chest, half anger, half defensive posture. Defiant tears slid down her cheeks. "I will never forgive you for this."

He laughed. "See, that's the thing, Persephone. I don't care. I don't require your approval or your love. I just want you to scream pretty for me again."

Before he could unlock the cage and drag her out of it, there was a thundering sound on the stairs. Both Persephone and Hades turned in the direction of the doorway to see a man . . . no, one of the under beings, race downstairs.

"Nick!" Hades said, jovially. "Did you come to watch me play with my sad little prisoner?"

Nick's eyes widened. He spared a brief worried glance to Persephone then turned his attention back to Hades. "I can't believe you really did it."

"Now, now. Where's the respect? Is this how you speak to me now?"

Nick bowed. "Forgive me, My Lord Hades."

"That's better. Now what has you racing down here like the flames of hell are after you?"

"Zeus knows."

Hades laughed, a deep thundering sound that caused Persephone's cage to rattle. "Well, of course he knows. You can't destroy a hundred souls without word getting around."

"I've just come from seeing him."

"And why would you do that?" Hades asked as if he wasn't truly concerned with the answer.

"He's ended winter and returned the balance. He wants to call a truce. He says he's willing to meet with you to make a deal regarding Persephone's release."

This only made Hades laugh louder. "Oh, he's *willing* to meet with me, is he? How gracious. Well I'm not willing to meet with him. I have everything I want. I don't need any deals. And Persephone isn't going anywhere. Ever."

"But My Lord . . ."

"Tell him it's done. He lost. I won. She is mine. And tell him not to test me again. If he restarts winter or does anything else to flood us with too many souls, I will start destroying them again, and the next time I won't stop at a mere hundred. He knows the more I destroy the less reasonable I become. And Persephone has to live with me. He needs to remember that."

Nick looked as though he might argue, but instead he sighed. "Yes, My Lord. I'll tell him."

"Good. Go now." Hades smiled at Persephone. "I have things to do."

Nick spared her one last worried glance. "Please, My Lord . . . don't hurt her. You'll regret it."

Hades moved in closer to Nick, and the under being took several steps back, losing his courage as soon as he'd found it.

"That might be true if the old me was coming back, but he isn't. We both knew there was no coming back from taking this many souls. This is the god of the underworld you're all stuck with now. You can thank Zeus for that. Now go!"

"Y-yes, My Lord." Nick scrambled out of the dungeon and up the stairs. His panicked footsteps quickly receded, leaving Persephone alone with the monster.

Hades walked in a slow circle around the cage. "I'm so excited. I can't decide what to do with you first."

Persephone huddled as far from him as she could get, tears streaming down her face. "Please, Master. You don't want to do this."

He sighed and stopped circling the cage. "Everyone seems to think they know what I want. What I want is to fuck you and hurt you. What I want is for you to be terrified of your lord and master. I want you to cower and beg and cry and scream for me. I want to watch you suffer and bleed. And I want to do it forever. It might even amuse me to send you down to Melos in the lower realms and let him show you what his real punishments are like."

She wanted to believe there was something of the Hades she'd known that she could still reach. There was the smallest similarity in the sound of his voice. There were a few facial features that if she looked very hard, she could still find him, but the person she'd known was gone. She'd been a little idiot to think he was scary when he'd first brought her down here. It was nothing to what he was now.

There was nothing to reach. She knew it. Her tears and pleading and pain wouldn't affect him as they had before. She'd lost him. Her sobs came out in earnest now.

"That won't help you. It doesn't affect me," he said.

She wouldn't tell him that her crying was for the man she lost, the one she'd loved. He would only laugh at her.

His voice was so cold, so dead when he spoke. His face didn't light up when he looked at her now. All she saw in his face was the triumph of winning and claiming a prize. That's all she was to him.

Suddenly Persephone felt something like cold clammy death in the pit of her stomach. Hades' touch and nearness was the only thing that had made the underworld bearable. And now she had to withstand this place and the monster who had replaced him? It was too much.

All she wanted now was freedom and escape. If the man she loved was lost, and all that remained was this terrible place, she just wanted to get out of it at any cost. But death wouldn't release her, and she knew Hades wouldn't.

Before she'd had the smallest hope he might find it within himself to let her return to the surface, that he would understand she couldn't live down here and take pity on her. Even if he didn't love her like she loved him, maybe he would feel *something* and let her go. Now that hope was gone because this creature wasn't letting her go anywhere.

The weight of the underworld pushed in on her again, the hopeless endless death of night. She felt like she was drowning in it, and that was just the place itself. She was so lost inside herself in this dreaded feeling that she didn't notice when the cage door creaked open and Hades stepped inside.

It wasn't until he gripped her arm and dragged her out that she realized what was happening.

But when he touched her . . . somehow against all reason, she felt the smallest balm of comfort. The underworld's power to hurt her fled in the face of his hands on her because he remained the master of this place no matter what form he took. Somehow, he could still give her peace even when he was the bigger threat—even when giving her peace wasn't his goal.

She didn't fight him when he pulled her out of the cage. Not only was it futile, but it was better to be with him anywhere than be left down here alone with the madness that overtook her when it was only her and the screaming void of the underworld.

Hades was silent as he carried her up the stairs to the main level. There was a palpable change in the air up here— something different in the stance of the guards and servants. They trembled in his presence. If they were scared of him now, what hope did she have? They'd never seemed scared of him before. Respectful and obedient, but not scared.

Even the castle itself seemed afraid.

Hades carried her up the grand staircase and then up to his floor. She knew where he was taking her before they got there. The playroom.

Once they were inside the room, he set her down on the ground.

"I owe you a punishment," he said.

But they both knew he wasn't punishing her for the secrets she'd kept or trying to hurt herself. He no longer cared about any of that. He just wanted to hurt her.

Persephone looked down at her wrists still wrapped in gauze. It seemed impossible that all of this had happened in the space of a day, that just this morning she'd loved the monster she now merely needed.

He gripped one of her wrists and unwrapped the gauze. He growled at the sight of her injury. Still too fresh.

"You're far too easy to damage." He pushed her away and she fell against the hard stone floor. "No matter, Sunshine, I'm sure I can find ways to hurt you that don't require long healing time. I can pace myself."

He raised an arm and the leather table came shooting out from the closet.

"Take off the robe," he practically snarled when he saw she was still dressed.

Persephone tried to drag it out, unlatching the silver clasps as slowly as she could manage, but Hades noticed, and the look he gave her had her rushing to undress.

"On the table."

She climbed up on the table, unable to stop trembling. She tried to reassure herself he wasn't going to do anything that required healing time. He wasn't going to seriously injure her. There were limits to what he could do. She'd survive it. She tried to push away the thoughts that kept crowding into her head reminding her this wasn't worth surviving. Going on like this wasn't worth it. And yet even death couldn't free her.

It was hopeless.

"Master . . . please."

"The more you beg, the more excited I get, so you might want to rethink that strategy." He moved closer to her, so close she could feel the heat coming off his skin. Then he bent and licked the tears off her face. "Fucking delicious," he said.

She leaned closer when his tongue dragged over her cheek. She shouldn't want him to touch her. But she couldn't help it. It calmed her. It shut up the screaming panic for as long as he touched her. It had to be some kind of magic, but if it was, it wasn't one he was consciously controlling. Comfort was the last thing he wanted to give her. He no longer seemed capable of it.

Then he pulled away, and the creeping dread was back. Persephone wished he'd just do whatever he was going to do. She couldn't stand this anticipation. She couldn't cope with the underworld *and* a monster bent on her destruction.

"M-Master. You won. You have me forever now. I know you'll never release me. But do you really want to break your favorite toy?"

He chuckled. "Not an expert negotiator, are you, Sunshine? Maybe I like my toys broken. How would you know? You've never met the real me. Until now."

He was lying. Whatever this was, this wasn't the real him. She closed her eyes against the memory of him inciner-ating that soul. He'd done that before he'd become this . . . thing.

Maybe he had always been worse than she'd imagined. Or maybe just desperate.

Hades took the ropes from under the leather table and tied her down spread-eagled on her stomach.

When he went for the whip, she started to cry. Before, it had been different. There had been someone who was in control of himself, who deep down she'd known didn't really want to hurt her. She'd grown used to seeing Hades as her protector down here. And now there was no one who could or would protect her from Hades.

Nine

Persephone felt numb. Hades had finally put the whip away. The hope she'd had that he wouldn't damage her was gone. She felt the blood dripping down her back. How would she survive him? If this was what he did the first day of the new him. There was nothing left of him.

She couldn't stop crying, and yet at the same time, it had become such a background noise that she could barely remember she was doing it. She cringed when he jumped on the table with her. It creaked under his weight.

She was afraid to beg him because she knew the more she reacted the more it drove him on. All conscience and feeling had left him. He might talk like a man, but he wasn't one. It was all just . . . empty inside.

Why couldn't Zeus have left well enough alone? Despite the suffocating energy of the underworld itself, she'd started to feel happy with Hades. She'd felt free. He'd been kind to her. It wasn't as though she knew Zeus or had even met him. Some father. All he cared about was controlling her. If he was any kind of real father he wouldn't have kept so much from her.

"Master, did you know you would become this if you destroyed those souls?"

"Yes. Everything was too complicated. And now . . . it isn't."

Maybe she could have forgiven him if he hadn't known what he would become. Even with the horror of it all. She could have decided to believe taking all those souls had been an act of desperation and temporary insanity, not premeditated pure evil.

She flinched when she felt his tongue on her back, lapping up the blood. All she wanted was to get away from him. And at the same time, all she wanted was to get closer. Because even after the pain he'd just caused her . . . even after breaking her skin and making her bleed and suffer, when he touched her, she was home and everything felt safe. She was the farthest she could be from safe, and yet despite the rational truth, all she wanted was for him to touch her. If only he'd leave the whip alone and put his hands on her.

A moan left her throat as his tongue moved over her skin.

"Even after everything I have done and will do to you, you still want me," he said.

No. Needed. But she couldn't tell him that. He truly *would* use it against her now.

He untied her and left her alone in the room. Several endless minutes passed, but before the screeching panic could claw its way to the surface, the door opened again and one of the female servants stepped in. It was the same girl who'd brought her food a few hours before.

"Your Grace," she said quietly, looking down at the ground.

"Please stop calling me that. We both know it's a lie. Just call me Persephone."

She shook her head. "Oh no, I can't call you that. It would be wrong. Disrespectful."

Persephone didn't bother fighting her on the issue. She was too exhausted. And in the grand scheme, the mockery of that title was the least of her troubles.

The servant carried a large basket filled with first aid supplies. She put it on the table and pulled the items out carefully one by one.

"Does he know you're doing this?"

The girl kept her eyes trained on the items from the basket. "He sent me. He wants you cleaned up and brought to him in his room."

A hard lump formed in Persephone's throat. They both knew what that meant. He'd beaten her. Now he wanted to fuck her. But he didn't want her blood messing up his nice sheets.

She started to cry.

"You must be brave, Your Grace," the servant girl said.

Persephone couldn't bring herself to explain the true cause of her tears. She wasn't crying because she was terrified or horrified by the idea of sleeping with him like this. It was the fact that she knew, even after everything, destroying souls, destroying her . . . she would like it. She'd found no evidence that any direct physical touch from him would or could ever repulse or upset her. Quite the contrary.

In his new form, everything was a thousand times worse. And yet he was both everything bad and everything good. He created all her suffering, and then his touch erased it all again so the miserable cycle could start all over.

The girl spread an ointment over the whip lashes on Persephone's back. "We aren't really much into healing things down here, but this might help you heal a little faster than normal."

She wasn't sure she wanted to heal a little faster. Healing faster only meant more would come sooner. But she didn't say anything. Hades had ordered this. The girl would carry it out. And there was nothing Persephone could do to thwart him.

The servant worked quietly applying the ointment and then the bandages. Below the sting, the whip had caused a painful ache. How long would it take that to heal, and would he spare her more pain until then? Or would he learn to work around her human frailties with pain that caused less damage?

A part of her still didn't believe she was a goddess. Wouldn't that be a fucked-up twist of fate . . . to have been the wrong girl this whole time?

But if Zeus had turned the world to winter to get her back, she must be who they said. Even if she didn't know herself, he did.

Once the bandages were secure, the girl opened the basket again and pulled out something slinky and shimmering. It was the dress Hades had ordered made for her for that first party—the night she'd first realized just how far she'd started to fall for him, the night she'd been truly awakened to a carnal potential she'd never known she had or wanted.

"No. Not that dress," she said.

"He wants this one. It has to be this one."

It was too painful remembering that night. The sharpest memory wasn't the endless hours of pleasure, it was when she'd gotten scared and Hades had pulled her out of there and taken care of her. She knew he'd never do anything like that again.

"Please, Your Grace. It will only be worse for you if you fight him on this."

Persephone knew she wouldn't fight him on anything. It would get her nothing but suffering. She allowed the servant to help her into the sheer gown without further complaint. When the girl was finished, she packed up the basket and left. On her way out the door she said, "You must go to him now. He's waiting."

Persephone paused outside the bedroom door and took a long, deep breath. The guard standing in the hallway looked at her with pity as if he wanted to rescue her from this fate. It felt as though every being in this castle wanted to rescue and help her, but none of them had the will to defy Hades.

And even if they did, it occurred to her that if he ruled the entire underworld, he had far more power than she'd ever witnessed or fully contemplated. Every being in this place had to know that to fight him would mean their own annihilation. He could destroy anyone or anything he wanted down here. Persephone hadn't appreciated just how much power he'd had and how much self-control, until he let go of it. She hadn't understood until now how safe and cherished she'd truly been in his arms.

Tears had been silently moving down her cheeks, but she couldn't stop the loud strangled sob that escaped her.

"I'm so sorry, Your Grace," the guard said. "We never thought that he would ever . . ."

"I know. It's not your fault."

And even if they had thought it, what were they going to do about it? They were all helpless actors on his stage. If that stage was a hedonistic orgy or a horror show of torment, either way, everything that happened in this realm happened at his pleasure.

She scrubbed the tears off her face with the back of her hand and pushed the door open.

Hades was in the bed, naked and waiting for her. Suddenly that enormous bed seemed only normal-sized with him inside it in his darker form. He motioned her forward, and she went to him. His eyes lit with a familiar desire, and all she wanted was to pretend that some part of the god she knew was still in there somewhere underneath the monster. She wanted to believe that he was fighting to get back to her.

"You still want me, I can feel it," he said.

She wanted to deny it. She wanted to fight and scream and run and be horrified—not because of the way he looked but because of the cold cruelty of this new form. She didn't want to believe she could want someone so callous. But she did still want him because when his hands were on her, even in this form, she could close her eyes and pretend it was him. Instead of this weak dark copy.

"Poor, lost Persephone," he said.

She stood mere inches from him now, well within his grasp. He ran his hands over the slinky shimmery dress, admiring her. When he touched her, even now, she had no will to try to escape him. All she wanted was more.

He moved a hand underneath the high slit in the dress and between her legs. She widened her stance to give him access and whimpered as he stroked her. He could so easily rip into her with those claws, but he was being careful for now.

"I knew you would still be wet for me."

He withdrew his hand.

"Master, please."

He chuckled and laid back against the pillows, moving the blankets out of their way. Persephone climbed onto the bed and pulled the fabric of the dress up. She straddled him, grateful he didn't seem intent to fuck her on her back with those fresh whip marks still searing into her skin.

She gasped when he filled her. That statue at the party had been exact. Except now instead of cold marble it was warm flesh that made her buzz with a euphoria that barely seemed possible. He didn't have to prompt or guide her. She closed her eyes and started to move on her own. But he was just so big.

He gripped her waist and helped raise and lower her at the pace he wanted.

"No," he said. "Look at me. I don't want you to pretend it's him."

Persephone opened her eyes and met his gaze. His eyes glowed that terrifying red, and it seemed as though he could burn her out of existence with only a look if he wanted. He probably could. But the way he looked at her was as intense as it had been in his previous form.

She touched the side of his face, looking for any part of him that might still exist deep inside.

Hades gripped her wrist and pulled her hand away. He growled. "No. Fuck me. We aren't going to make love."

And yet, he wanted eye contact. He didn't want to fuck her from behind so she could pretend whatever she wanted. He claimed he only wanted to fuck, but he wouldn't allow distance between them.

Even in this form, how could she see it as anything other than making love—despite the emotions he didn't seem capable of? There was no elaborate kink. They were in a bed, looking into each other's eyes, languidly moving together in an ancient dance that didn't feel like just fucking.

His hands on her, his gaze on her, his cock inside her made her want to stay in this moment forever. She never wanted to leave this bed. She never wanted to have to face his cold distance, or that whip or his chains, or the casual cruelty of his words.

After a small eternity, the pleasure inside her began to build.

"Yes, give yourself to the monster who destroyed the man you loved. Come for me."

His words hurt with equal intensity as the pleasure and peace of his hands on her body. But she couldn't stop it now. She let go and allowed the pleasure to flow over her. If this was her life now, shouldn't she have just a little pleasure to edge out the pain?

"Good girl," he said when she laid against his chest, spent.

He gripped her ass and thrust harder and faster into her until he reached his own peak All she could do was hold onto him.

And then it was over. He didn't cuddle with her. He didn't stroke her hair. He just pulled out of her and got out of the bed and quietly put his pants back on.

Persephone lay huddled in the bed, crying. She felt like she was cheating on him with him—taking comfort in something that wasn't even real. Hades put a hand on her shoulder. She didn't want to lean into that touch, but she did, unable to resist any small peace he offered her.

"He's never coming back, Sunshine. Accept it. I'm the one you need to concern yourself with pleasing now."

Ten

I t had only been a few days, but to Persephone it felt as though thousands of years had passed. Time held no meaning. The watch Hades had given her was pointless. Nothing mattered anymore. What difference did it make if she knew what time it was in New York? That life was over.

She didn't know what was happening on the surface, but the cold, dead winter seemed to have left the earth and come to the underworld. Everything felt more cold and dead than it ever had. There was nothing but fear here anymore.

Hades sat on the large throne-like chair in the ballroom. The candles were all lit. Everything gleamed as if for a party. But there was no party—just scared guards, scared servants, scared under beings . . . and her.

Persephone was nude, kneeling on a cushion at Hades' feet. He'd attached a heavy chain to her collar. The other end was bolted into the floor next to his chair. Hades dragged his claw lightly along the back of her neck. He knew and she knew that if he pressed just the tiniest bit, he would draw blood.

He liked to keep her there on the very edge of blood and pain, poised between anxiety and peace.

Her back was still bandaged from his last punishment, but it hurt less. That hadn't stopped him from devising other ways to hurt and scare her in the days in between. She'd learned in a short time that being suspended by ropes for hours could hurt just as much as a whip, but it didn't require healing time.

She'd learned he could get inside her head and torment her mind in ways that went beyond any physical pain he could devise.

The ballroom doors opened, and Melos burst in. His gaze went briefly to Persephone, and he flinched. The only thing worse than what Hades had become was everyone else's useless pity for her.

"How dare you burst in here without an invitation?" Hades said. His voice was calm and polite, but the barely constrained rage bubbled just below the surface so palpable everyone in the room could feel it on the air. He would take this out on her later. He always took everybody else's fuck-ups out on her.

"M-my Lord, Hades, I apologize." Melos was shaking.

This terrifying under being in charge of torture in the lower realms was shaking. Every time Persephone witnessed this kind of reaction from one of his generals or even one of the servants or guards, her heart sank a little further because she was beginning to realize he *was* being lenient with her. He'd destroyed two under beings in the space of a day for bringing him news he didn't find pleasing. If he was being lenient with her, what happened when the newness wore off and she was just another thing to hurt?

As cold and cruel as he was, the way he was with Persephone was his *good* side now.

"What do you want?" Hades said, his claws clicking impatiently on the arm rest.

"I beg your pardon, My Lord, but there is a matter of some urgency happening right outside the castle in the garden."

Hades raised an eyebrow. "Oh? Who would dare to create a problem on the grounds of my home? My, but we all do seem to have an annihilation wish now, don't we?"

"Please, you must come."

Hades sighed, rose from his chair, and followed the general outside. A few moments after the ballroom doors shut, they opened again, but this time it was Nick. He carried an ancient-looking jar with reverence and care as if it contained the key to all life. When he spotted Persephone, he rushed across the ballroom to her side.

He knelt next to her. "Your Grace, we don't have a lot of time before he comes back. You must drink this."

Nick thrust the jar into her hands. It was warm like the sun. There were strange etchings on the exterior. She didn't know what they meant, but they felt powerful like they had existed from the beginning.

"W-what is it?"

"Your powers. Zeus gave them to me to give to you. You must drink it now. This might be your only chance."

Persephone unscrewed the lid and smelled the contents of the jar. It didn't smell like anything, but the liquid inside glowed pale pink. She felt sure the glowing couldn't be good. What if it was some kind of trick? Or a test? She'd learned that Nick was Hades' most trusted spy. What if it was a test to see if she would do something to defy him?

But what if it wasn't? Nick seemed far too scared to be part of some grand plan to destroy her.

Despite her fears, all she could think was this might somehow help her withstand Hades. She closed her eyes and drank the contents of the jar. It tasted like spring rain and sunflowers and apple blossoms and sunlight and butterflies and wriggling caterpillars. It tasted like hope and second chances and beginnings. It tasted like safety and warmth and home.

The pink glow moved through her, and she felt so . . . strong. Indestructible. Ancient. Enduring. Was this how Hades and Zeus felt all the time? Was this what had been stolen and hidden from her?

Then the real magic started. Suddenly, she knew. Everything. She knew how all things had been from the foundations of the world. She knew who she was. What she was. There was no longer any doubt. She knew Zeus had been using her stolen powers to awaken the world in Springtime.

She felt alive in ways she'd never before felt. Even the darkness of the underworld couldn't crush her. The long, unyielding sadness left her, and now she just felt strong.

She no longer needed Hades to touch her to make her feel like she wasn't dying, because now she felt more alive than ever before. And she understood.

She understood darkness and death and pain and destruction, because out of those things her powers brought life and hope and growing things. Out of the darkest, deadest winter, spring always came back. And she felt compassion for the dead and hopeless things. Even for Hades. She'd thought she loved him before, but now she could see and understand and feel him in ways she couldn't have comprehended before.

No longer did she reason and think and feel like a human, but like a god. She didn't process what he'd done as a human would. With her more human feelings she might not have been capable of forgiving him for destroying souls. As a goddess it felt . . . different, still wrong, but . . . different. She felt his desperation and pain and the need to keep her.

She didn't just know who she was. She knew who everyone was, who Hades was—the pain and loneliness and despair he'd carried until he'd found her. The bitterness and resentment of the lot he'd drawn. The injustice of the one being who might make his life bearable being kept from him. And in that moment, she forgave him.

"Your Grace?" Nick had a worried expression on his face.

She had sort of left them all there for a moment. Persephone gave the jar back to Nick.

"How do you feel?" he asked as if concerned the transfer hadn't taken.

She smiled. "Like a goddess. Like the queen."

When she looked along the walls at the guards and servants, she saw and felt the slightest shift in them from fear . . . to hope.

There were sounds out in the hallway. Nick scrambled to get off the ground and bolted out a side entrance. That was probably wise. Hades would destroy him if he knew what he'd done.

Moments later, the door was flung open, and Hades stepped into the ballroom, his eyes glowing bright red. He blazed across the floor to Persephone, the rage crackling and rolling off him, electrifying the air like a static charge. For a moment, she thought he'd caught Melos and Nick at their deception. But if that were true, he would have sent guards after them or looked around the ballroom for Nick. There was no indication he realized his spy had been there in his absence.

Maybe he knew Persephone had changed. Could he feel it?

He detached the chain from her collar and jerked her up off the ground, dragging her without a word out of the ballroom, down the hallway, up the stairs, to the playroom. He didn't pause to acknowledge her until he had her chained the way he wanted: standing, legs and arms spread wide, much like Melos had her at her introduction party.

Hades towered over her, his arms crossed over his massive chest. "I don't care how healed you are. I want to hurt you."

"Master, did I do something to displease you?"

He snorted. "No, Persephone. You are as sweet and lovely as ever. Your behavior is perfect and has nothing to do with the things I want to do to you."

Hades stepped behind her and ripped her bandages off. He let out a surprised gasp and ran his fingertips—claws lightly dragging—across her back. "Something's not right. The ointment shouldn't have worked this well or this quickly."

Persephone remained silent, her breath already coming out in frightened pants.

He went to the closet and returned with his favorite whip. The leather cut through the air only a moment before it cut through her, drawing fresh cries from deep within her. If she'd thought having her powers back would make this hurt less, she'd been very wrong about that. It was still the same stinging fire across her back.

"What?" He said, confused. "This can't be."

"W-what can't be?"

"You just healed. I broke your skin, and then it healed. Instantly." Hades circled around her again and came to stand in front of her. He gripped her throat so hard, she feared he'd break her neck—not that she could die. But pain was still pain, and far from muting everything, getting her powers had only made everything louder, brighter, sharper. Now when he hurt her, she didn't only feel her own pain, she felt his, too. It was the kind of pain that could swallow the world.

"What. Did. You. Do?" he growled.

It was the first time he'd been officially displeased with her since the transformation. For a moment, the fear of just how awful he might become swamped her. He released her throat and took a couple of steps back.

"Well? Speak."

She wouldn't give Nick away. But Hades must know. Who else could it be? It suddenly occurred to her that Nick had known all along this might be a suicide mission because there was no hiding her powers from Hades or anyone else for long. The under being may have sacrificed his existence for her.

"I have my powers back," she said unnecessarily.

"I know that. How?"

Persephone didn't answer.

"No matter. I should be grateful. This just makes you more . . . durable. There are so many things I've wanted to do to you. But your annoyingly slow healing time got in the way. I've been so impatient to hurt you just a little more . . . never satisfied with the limits of your fragility." He leaned in close and whispered, "Still, I've loved that I can fuck you knowing no matter what I do to you, your body will always want me. Whoever gave you your powers back must really hate you."

His anger was replaced with a buzz of excitement as if all his wishes and dreams were impossibly coming true. He went back to the closet, tossing things out behind him in a frenzy until he found the box he wanted. It was dark wood with intricate carvings and fit easily in his enormous hands.

He opened the box to show her the contents. Persephone's eyes widened.

"Tell me, Sunshine . . . do you like knives?"

She hadn't wanted to whimper and beg, knowing it would only drive him on, but she couldn't help the tears that started moving down her cheeks, the fear she now knew he could feel and practically taste. There had been little point in being brave. He knew what she felt just as she knew what he felt.

"Master, please."

"I was wondering when you'd beg for me." He set the box on the ground and took out one of the knives. He laid the flat of the blade gently against the side of her cheek. "You know I can do the same damage with claws. I'll tell you what . . . lady's choice . . . claws or knives?"

She rattled the chains. "Master, please unchain me."

His eyes lit with malicious glee. "And why would I do that when I like you so scared and helpless?"

"Y-you don't really like me this way."

He prowled around her, sniffing, inhaling her fear. "I'm pretty sure I do."

"But you didn't . . . before you changed."

He growled. "That was then. This is now." He stopped prowling and stood still as if lost in thought. "You know what? I *am* going to take you down out of the chains. I'm going to take you to the ballroom and hurt you there. We'll let everyone watch the helpless destruction of the queen of the underworld. Would you like that, Sunshine?"

She flinched when he stroked the side of her cheek.

"Oh, that's right. You don't need me to touch you anymore to cope with the underworld. But I bet I can still make you wet for me. I think I should do it downstairs with an audience. I know how you love an audience."

Persephone didn't respond. If she appeared too eager, he'd know something was up.

"I-I'm sorry, Master."

"Too late. I like my new plan." He unchained her.

Persephone stepped closer to him. "My poor, lost Hades," she said sadly.

He growled. "Don't you dare pity and patronize me. I will make you regret that," he snarled.

"No, you won't. The rules of the game have changed."

You had to love them, or the spark of life wouldn't come back.

Persephone reached up and touched the side of his face. She poured every ounce of compassion and love and power she had into him. She was certain that even if she still thought and felt like a human, she would love him if it was the price necessary to bring him back because this wasn't about what she needed. It was how she'd always brought things back, and now she knew why. Even without her powers in the human realm, some small bit of magic must have clung to her, the slightest essence of who she was.

Hades gripped her wrist and jerked her hand away from his face. "What do you think you're doing, Sunshine?"

"Bringing you back to life."

It was too late for him to stop her. It was already done. A massive light filled the room, making it so hot and bright even she wasn't sure she could withstand it. After several minutes, both the heat and light faded. Hades lay naked and trembling in the center of the room, his beautiful human form returned.

He sobbed uncontrollably.

Persephone went to him and knelt beside him, pulling him into her arms, stroking his hair. "Everything will be okay now, Master."

He cringed when she called him that as if it were some sort of strange punishment she'd devised to torment him.

"You trusted me and I . . ."

"It wasn't you," she said.

"Like hell it wasn't me. It was me. It was just a me that didn't have to care how much I hurt you or how many souls I destroyed. I could have what I wanted without any consequences. The things I said to you . . . The things I *did* to you . . ." Broken sobs punctuated every few words as he tried to speak past them. "I know you can't ever forgive me."

Persephone still held him, afraid if she let go he might crumble apart. He seemed so uncharacteristically breakable. It was so strange being the strong one. She didn't like it at all. "Shhhh no more crazy talk. I already forgave you. I'm just glad you came back to me."

Though she could withstand the dark energy of the underworld now without pain, she still missed the sunlight on her skin and growing things. Although she was a goddess, she missed the simple humanity she'd lived. That life was a lie . . . just like all the other lies she'd lived for thousands of years as her father had messed with her memories to keep her hidden. But it didn't matter anymore.

It wasn't only that she missed the human world. The issue was bigger now. And now was probably the only shot she had to make Hades listen to reason.

"Master, you have to let me go to the surface," she said gently. He tensed in her embrace. As much remorse as he felt, he still couldn't let her go without a fight. "I have my powers back. That comes with responsibilities. The earth will die if I never go up there again."

He was silent for several minutes then let out a long defeated sigh. "I'll arrange a meeting with Zeus."

She leaned down and whispered in his ear. "I will always belong to you. I don't want what we had before you went away to change. I like who I became with you. I just can't be in the underworld all the time."

"I know. I think I always knew."

Eleven

Hades sat next to Persephone at a glass table in a long, white conference room. The walls were plain with nothing taped or hanging on them. Around the table were twelve comfortable high-backed black leather swivel chairs. Hades sat at the head of the table with Persephone in a chair beside him.

"What did you say this place was again?" she asked.

"It's just a meeting place inside the neutral zone," Hades said staring at the door at the other end.

"Neutral zone?"

He finally turned to look at her. "Yes, it's a place that is safe for both underworld beings and upper world beings. Some of us can walk between the worlds, but not all of us can. It's the only way Zeus and I can be in the same place for long enough to have a real conversation. I think a lot of the mortals now call it something like purgatory."

All she said was, "Oh."

Hades wasn't an idiot. He knew Zeus had tricked him— sending Persephone's powers back to her like that.

It was the ace he'd had up his sleeve the whole time, and Hades hadn't seen it coming. He'd been too lost inside the freedom of not caring about anything, too lost inside the monster.

If he kept her in the underworld, and the world died . . . it was too many souls to process, and he'd sworn to Persephone he'd never destroy so many souls like that again. After she'd restored him, he'd spent hours crying in her arms like a big baby. If his generals could have seen him. If Zeus could have seen him. Just lying there, broken on the floor. Not his finest moment.

He still couldn't believe she'd forgiven him. Destroying those souls was bad enough, but the more personal things . . . That was something inside him he'd never wanted her to know. There was always the dark urge. How far would he have taken things if she hadn't gotten her powers back so quickly?

"This place is more disturbing than the underworld," she said. "I feel like Betty from accounting is gonna come in with a cup of stale coffee in a paper cup for banal small talk while endless filing goes on in the background behind her." She put her hand over Hades'.

He chuckled. She always had a way of bringing him out of bad places. She may have forgiven him, but he wasn't sure he could ever forgive himself. It was why he had to do this for her. It wasn't about his rivalry with Zeus or about how he'd been tricked. It was about what he owed her for saving him in a million tiny ways, for being more than he ever could have hoped for. Much more than he deserved.

Recessed into the ceiling were a row of irritating fluorescent lighting fixtures. One of them was blinking. It had that buzzing bug zapper quality to it. Persephone was right. This place was more disturbing then the underworld.

"What's going to happen?" she asked.

He could feel the nervous energy buzzing off her, mirroring the buzz of the flicking light. "We're just going to talk."

After several long minutes, the door opened and in walked Zeus. He'd always looked both very young and very old at the same time. He wore a loose white T-shirt, and long shorts that had brightly colored flowers on them.

He was tan with brilliant green eyes that seemed even more bright next to the glow of that tan. He had flowing white hair and a white beard, but other than the hair he looked about thirty. He smelled like tanning oil, the scent wafting gently throughout the conference room.

Zeus looked sadly at Persephone and shook his head. "My sweet, darling daughter, what has this monster done to you?"

Persephone scooted her chair closer to Hades. "At least he didn't hide my powers and identity from me. At least he let me find my real self instead of endless lies."

Hades felt the smirk inch up the side of his face. This meeting might not be so terrible after all. He wished he could bottle Zeus's anger. The other god looked like he might turn into a ball of fire and explode right then and there, leaving a scorch mark on the light gray corporate-friendly carpet.

"You're late," Hades remarked.

"I was in Bermuda enjoying the sun." He'd no doubt made a beeline for the beach the moment he fixed the earth. Zeus hated winter just as much as everyone else did.

"Must be nice. I keep hearing about this thing you call the sun, but it never wants to come out when I'm on the surface."

"Sorry about that," Zeus said, sitting in the chair at the opposite end of the table from them.

Hades frowned. "No, you're not. And yet, I somehow have managed to acquire the only sunlight that matters." He trailed his fingertips along Persephone's arm.

"Enough!" Persephone shouted, pulling away from him. She stood and crossed her arms over her chest. "I'm not some meaty bone for you dogs to fight over! Stop discussing me like I'm not even in the room."

Zeus looked taken aback by her outburst, but she didn't seem to care.

"I'm not the same coddled and sheltered child you carted all over the planet and kept naive. I'm a grown woman and a goddess with a consort of my own. I'm the queen of the underworld, goddammit!"

Hades laughed. Zeus flinched—probably over that consort part. But Persephone wasn't done.

"I'm not some object you two can negotiate over. Don't either of you care what the hell I want?"

"We know what you want," Zeus said. "You want to be free of him."

Hades looked down at the table, the mirth of only seconds ago, gone. He could feel her eyes on him. He couldn't look at her because deep down he knew that must be true. He'd taken her from her life and sentenced her to be his forever. Of course she wanted to be free of him.

"No. I just want to go home. I have work to do."

"To Olympus?" Zeus asked, raising a white eyebrow.

"NO!" She practically growled when she said it. Hades looked up just in time to see her eyes glow bright blue. "My home! In New York. I want to go back to my apartment over the Chinese restaurant and my plants. I want my job back. I want my friends back. I want the sun and rain and wind. I want to be among the *living*."

Hades flinched.

"So you want to be free of him," Zeus said.

She sank back into her chair. "That's *not* what I said. I swear, neither one of you listens."

"Hades, don't you think it's time you let her go?"

"She can't go. She ate the seeds," Hades said. Zeus thought he was the only one with an ace. Hades had to keep reminding himself that those pomegranate seeds would always tie her to him, one way or another. She could never be completely free of the underworld.

"How many?" Zeus pressed.

Hades continued to stare at the table as if he could burn a hole through it by sheer force of will. "Six," he said finally.

"Ah, well, that's easy then. So you know the solution. You've always known it. You can't be on the surface that long, but she can. It's a compromise we can all try to live with."

Hades glared at Zeus. "And what makes you think I'll let her go? Maybe you can extract her powers again and then . . ." He was being crazy, and everybody at the table knew it. But Zeus had seen more than he should.

"Because you love her," the other god said.

There was a long, silent moment.

Hades sighed. "I do."

"Then it's settled. I'll alter the memories of the mortals so things are as they were, and Persephone spends half the year on the surface . . ." he made a disgusted face, " . . . and half the year with you."

Persephone's hand slammed down on the table. "Hey. Still sitting right here, guys."

Zeus turned to her. "I'm sorry, Persephone. Is this plan agreeable to you?" He didn't really sound that sorry.

"Yes," she said quietly. "I just like to be asked."

Zeus rolled his chair back from under the desk, stood, and stretched. "Well, kids, I ordered a Surf 'n' Turf at the fish fry place down on the beach. It'll be out any minute now. I will send an emissary to arrange the details. Agreed, Hades?"

Hades sighed. "Agreed."

"Persephone?"

"Yes," she said.

"Good then. Well, this was one of our more productive meetings, I think." Zeus crossed to their end of the table and took Persephone's hand and kissed the back of it. "It was lovely to more formally meet you, my dear. I hope we'll talk again soon."

Before either she or Hades could respond he'd turned and left them alone in the room.

Persephone sighed. "I still don't understand why you can't live on the surface with me. Why can I be in the underworld but you can't be on the surface? It's so stupid."

The only way she'd fully understand was with a demonstration. "Close your eyes and extend your powers out into the room," Hades said.

Persephone closed her eyes. After a few moments, she glowed with a brilliant pale pink light. Plants began to sprout up everywhere. Trees grew from the center of the desk. Budding, blossoming, sprouting fruit.

"Now open your eyes," he said.

She opened her eyes, a look of wonder on her face as she took in the spectacle before her. She walked around the room, and everything came to life even more in her presence. Everything buzzed and hummed.

"It's all talking to me," she said. "I feel everything linked together inside me."

Rose bushes sprouted up in the corners, blossoming in pink and red and yellow blooms.

Hades rose from his chair and walked the perimeter of the room. As he passed, it all shriveled and died. Apples fell off trees, turned dark, and rotted in seconds. The roses lost all their petals which curled in on themselves and dried within moments before crumbling into a fine dust. Then there was nothing left but blackened twisted vines and thorns. Everything stopped humming and buzzing, and the whole room went still and quiet.

Hades moved closer to Persephone and took her into his arms. "This is why we can't be together on the surface. It's not just that I physically can't stay. Even if I could, this would be what the world would be like. And you would be just as unhappy. Death goes wherever I go. And life goes where you go. Except the underworld because I rule it. This is the only way we can maintain the balance."

Hades brushed a stray strand of blonde hair from her face. "I'll take you back home when you're ready."

Persephone stood with Hades out in the rain just outside the flower shop. He bent to kiss her, and she felt something like panic welling up in her chest. All of a sudden, she hated this plan. She wanted to be in the underworld with him.

She wrapped her arms around his neck, trying to hold onto his kiss longer, trying to remember his scent, the way he tasted, the softness of his lips on hers. Finally, he pulled away.

This was how it had to be. She would live half the time in the world she loved and half the time with the man she loved. Eventually, even with her powers, the underworld would wear on her, but for several months at a time, it was a workable solution. But why did leaving him now have to be so hard?

"You should go. I'll be back for you in six months. Enjoy the sun and your flowers," he said.

She could see in his eyes that he hated this plan just as much as she did. How could they be so right and so wrong for each other at the same time?

"Yeah. Sun," she said, glancing up at the dark sky. She was getting drenched standing out here in the pouring rain.

"You have to have some rain or nothing grows, you know. There will be plenty of sun. The sky can't help itself with you." He brushed the wet strands of hair from her face. "Go on."

"Are you sure they won't remember me gone?"

"Zeus took care of it. As far as Lynette remembers you haven't been missing."

"What about the man I thought was my father?"

"The same. Everything is as it should be. Go."

She started to cry. At first, she thought she could hide it from him with all the rain, but he knew.

"Persephone. Don't make this more difficult. You can't live for eternity in the dark. It's not right."

But she only cried harder.

Hades shook his head. "My poor, sweet goddess."

She looked up at him and laughed. "Not so sweet anymore."

"Yes. That's my influence." He wiped the tears off her face. "Go. Grow your flowers. Lie in the sunlight. Eat some of that amazing Italian sausage for me. Read books. Swim in the ocean. I'll be back for you soon enough. I'll always come for you, you know that."

Somehow, in the underworld, she'd grown accustomed to being his, but ever since getting her powers and the meeting with Zeus, it all felt as if it were falling apart and being taken away from her. She didn't want to lose that feeling of peace and safety—of him in control. He'd awakened things inside her that she wanted to keep. The only thing that remained to give any of it reality was the silver collar. Surely it meant something that it was still locked around her throat.

"Am I still yours?"

"Always, Sunshine. And when you return, I'll have devised all sorts of deviant punishments to make you pay for your recent sass."

She laughed. "Promise?"

"Oh, yes."

"And will there be parties?"

"You'll beg for them to stop," he promised. "Now quit stalling."

Hades pressed a kiss against her forehead, and then he turned and left. His long coat billowed behind him in the rain as he crossed the street.

Persephone reluctantly turned and went into the flower shop. The flowers perked up as she passed, buds opening, blooms going fuller, an extra burst of fragrance filling the room. She hoped Lynette didn't notice, but her boss had been engrossed in a different show.

"So. I didn't know you had a boyfriend," Lynette said. "Were you ever going to tell me about Mr. Tall, Dark, and Delicious?"

"You'd never believe the story." And if she did, she'd probably try to get Persephone to file a restraining order.

Persephone watched out the window as Hades started another black car that wasn't his car and pulled out into the rain. She watched until the sedan disappeared around a corner onto another street. She wanted to go after him, but he was right, she couldn't live forever in the dark, and she had her own responsibilities on the surface.

She had to find a way not to miss him too much. And when he came for her, she'd have to find a way to remember she would have light again.

As soon as he was out of sight, the rain stopped. The clouds seemed to melt into a brilliant blue sky, and the sun came out bright and warm.

Lynette stepped up behind her. "Well, would you look at that? It looks like it's going to be a beautiful sunny spring day after all."

Imagine that.

Late that afternoon while Lynette was out running errands, a delivery came. A fruit basket full of pomegranates sat outside on the front stoop. Persephone stepped out of the shop and looked around but saw no delivery truck. A cawing sound drew her attention to a nearby tree where a black raven stared down at her and tilted his head to the side.

She carried the basket into the shop and opened the card.

Something to remember me by. Don't worry, they came from your world, not mine.

She squeezed her eyes shut for a moment to keep the tears from spilling out. He would be back, and everything would be fine.

She opened the door again and looked up at the raven. "Well? Are you coming in?"

He cawed again and flew inside to perch on the table beside the basket. Persephone retrieved a knife from the break room and cut open one of the pomegranates. When she sliced it, the juice dripped out to stain the table. She'd thought she never wanted to see or taste another pomegranate seed again, but with Hades gone, it made him feel close.

She ate one of the sweet, juicy seeds. The flavors burst out on her tongue just as she'd remembered. When nothing tragic happened, she ate several more.

CPSIA information can be obtained
at www.ICGtesting.com
Printed in the USA
LVHW091943180719
624553LV00001B/4/P

9 781938 639388